Made for Two Rivals

MADISON HAYES

ELLORA'S CAVE
ROMANTICA PUBLISHING

What the critics are saying...

℀

5 Quills and a Must Read! *"Made for Two Rivals* is the second book in the *Made for Two* series and is a definite keeper. One of the best ménages that I have ever read, it fairly drips with a hot pulsing sexual overtone. But it is the emotional entanglements that reel you in and keep you eagerly glued page after page. [...] *Made for Two Rivals* is a must read that I highly recommend to everyone!" *~ www.gottawrittenetwork.com Reviews*

"Madison Hayes' latest Sci-fi work is not only fascinating, but is also decadent to boot. Using just the right pinch of romance with a blend of eroticism and worldly adventures, she created three characters with their own special uniqueness and made them work as a whole. [...] Great story and can't wait for the next addition to the *Made for Two* series." *~ Fallen Angels Reviews*

"Madison Hayes has written an excellent Sci-Fi erotic romance that will have you asking, where can I sign-up for Spaceforce! I know I want to know. The characters are very likeable, I found myself rooting for them. The sex scenes are Hot! There is M/F/M ménage action, but is in no way homoerotic. I look forward to the next book from this author." *~ ParaNormal Romance Reviews*

An Ellora's Cave Romantica Publication

www.ellorascave.com

Made For Two Rivals

ISBN 9781419959141
ALL RIGHTS RESERVED.
Made for Two Rivals Copyright © 2007 Madison Hayes
Edited by Pamela Campbell.
Cover art by Syneca.

This book printed in the U.S.A. by Jasmine–Jade Enterprises, LLC.

Electronic book Publication March 2007
Trade paperback Publication June 2009

MADE FOR TWO RIVALS

છા

Dedication

☙

For great friend and clever author, Dawn Madigan.

Chapter One

ɛɔ

Graham Hamm, more commonly known as the Hammer, sauntered into the officers' mess hall at Earth Base Ten. Like a fish on a line, his lazy gaze was attached to Bellamy Anders' ass as he followed the attractive brunette through the wide double doors. She had a nice derriere. He should know. Been there. Done that. Dragging his gaze from the provocative bounce of Bellamy's bottom, Gray scanned the rows of tables for his friends. After homing in on Matchstick's telltale slash of red hair, he veered left to join his wing companions. As he grinned at Jason, a flash of pale sunshine caught at the corner of his eye. The next thing he knew, Gray was tripping all over his own heavily booted feet.

Wise enough to know when he was pushing his limits, Gray stopped in the middle of the mess hall, giving his feet a chance to catch up to the rest of him. The rest of him was gawping. It wasn't only that his jaw was hanging—which it was. His body stiffened as every single one of his muscles knotted in preparation for action, much as it would in battlespace. In fact, the only difference he could ascertain lay in the behavior of his cock, which in point of detail wasn't behaving.

He held his breath and tilted his head as he narrowed his eyes on the woman who'd caught his attention—caught it and taken it hostage. She sat alone at the table behind the one at which his friends sat. And she was beautiful. Beautiful in a unique sense. Certainly not what you'd call pretty and not exactly sexy, either. Just…stunning. The way a suitcase full of money is stunning. Take-your-breath-away stunning.

Like a long-stemmed orchid, her appearance was slender and fragile. She looked as though a strong gust of wind would

9

bend her in two. Her long pale hair hung to the middle of her back in a straight wash of sunshine, framing a face both elegant and delicate. It was a long, heart-shaped face with a small pointed chin below a wide, full mouth and straight nose. Her huge amethyst eyes were expressive below shapely eyebrows. Just looking at her, Gray knew she could say a lot with those eyes. And what she could do with that mouth, he planned to discover in due time.

Gray, along with the other three members of his wing, had checked into Regional Command for their biennial training. After two years in space, the men were looking forward to their three-month stint on solid ground, not to mention the chance for a little full gravity sex. Sex in space was greatly overrated. You could never really plant and thrust. It just wasn't the same. And Gray was dominant in bed. He didn't like zero gravity. In space you could never tell who the fuck was on top.

Willing his feet back into motion, Gray stepped around a white-clad waiter 'droid and moved toward Jason and the others.

"Alpha Tango," he announced, uttering the two words that were guaranteed to silence his friends. The four men had been together since they'd entered the Spaceforce academy eight years ago. The two-word code was their private call to attention. Generally used as an alert, often in battle or under some threat, the words were occasionally uttered just before one of them had some earth-shattering information to impart.

"That's it, men. I'm in love." Gray dropped onto the bench seat opposite Jason and Matchstick. On his left, Jed slid over an aloof six inches. The Cajun liked his space. The Cajun was fucking antisocial when you got right down to it.

Jason took a swig of water, tipping his glass against his lips as he swiveled his head, following his friend's gaze. In the next instant, water sprayed from Jason's nose. "No, you're not!" he choked and sputtered, coughing and blinking back tears.

10

Gray checked his reflection on the smooth surface of the stainless steel table. He scraped a hand back through his straight black hair, trying to bring it under command. The thick brush slid around his fingers and somehow ended up back on his forehead again. Gray scowled down at the table, watching as his gunmetal eyes clouded to a stormy gray. He flicked his gaze to the girl, then back to Jason. "Would you mind telling me *why* I'm not?"

Jason leaned forward over the table. His tangled blond hair swept his collar as he lowered his voice. "That's Velvet Meadows." When Gray failed to react, Jason went on. "*The* Velvet Meadows. You know. The girl who walked into her dorm room and found a senior officer raping her roommate. She pulled the guy's dagger from his waistband and made a small cut behind his ear. Opened his vein and killed him as neat as slitting an envelope."

Gray's eyes widened. "You're kidding," he growled in a low rasp.

Jason shook his head.

"An officer? How'd she know...it was rape? I mean, how'd she know for certain they weren't just...?"

Jason shrugged. "There was an inquest but she was cleared. Turned out the guy *was* raping her roommate. Her roomie dropped out of the Force. I think the poor girl was as much rattled by the guy dying on top of her as she was by the rape itself. At any rate, nobody will share a room with Meadows anymore. She's in one of those tiny single dorms." Jason's voice dropped to a secretive murmur. "They say she never laughs. She hardly ever cracks a smile."

"She smiles in target practice," Jed informed the group. His voice was bored. His gaze was disinterested but nonetheless firmly pinned on the lovely little blonde.

Gray fingered the copper communicator that hugged the shell of his ear. "Who's fucking her?" he asked. Beside him, Jed grimaced. Gray ignored Jed's disapproval. "Anyone?"

Jason shook his head. "No one that I know of. She spends most of her time alone in her room."

Matchstick joined in, his voice no louder than Jason's. "She's crazy," he hissed. "I have Evasive Maneuvers with her. You should see her. Polyrounds going off all around her and she doesn't even blink. They say she was at Etiens."

Gray frowned at Match. "Etiens? I didn't think anyone *survived* Etiens. I thought the Grundians leveled the base. Didn't the blitz go on for…ninety days?"

Matchstick threw a furtive glance back over his shoulder toward the elegant blonde. Together, he and Jason nodded. "There were a few survivors. They just weren't much good for anything afterward. Most of them are still in repo."

"I'm not surprised," Jed put in without bothering to lower his voice. "Nobody can take that kind of punishment without going crazy."

Jason threw a look of cautious awe over his shoulder then returned his gaze to Gray. "She rode it out. Helped the rescue team dig out the survivors, dusted off her hands and went back into the smashed bunker to retrieve a notebook. She climbed back into that hellhole to get a *notebook*." He nodded significantly as he whispered, "Cool as chipped ice. Hard as diamonds."

"Jeezis," Gray breathed. "We've all had Psych Warfare. Didn't they tell us that no one can take that sort of stress without going nuts? Didn't they tell us it wasn't possible?"

Jed was just gazing at her from half-closed eyes. His mouth was a thin line. "It's not. Unless you're already nuts."

"What do you mean?"

The Cajun turned his green gaze on Gray. With one hand, he pushed a wavy strand of brown hair behind his ear. "The only ones who survive that sort of physical and mental assault are the ones who are already crazy."

"Jeezis," Gray whispered again. As the four men stared at the dainty young woman, she raised her gaze and locked it on

Gray. Her huge eyes blinked slowly before she lifted her palm to her lips and blew him a kiss.

Jason and Match turned their heads quickly to stare at Gray. Stunned silence followed.

With his gaze attached to hers, Gray groaned. He reached between his legs to rearrange his stiffening erection. "Crazy or not," he intoned in a low voice, "I'm gonna fuck that girl…if it's the last thing I do."

Jason and Match turned back to look at her. Jed's somnolent gaze never wavered.

The young woman gave the men a slow, sultry smile. They stared spellbound as she pushed back from her table and sauntered toward them. Without understanding why, the young officers rose to their feet.

Like the rest of the officers in the mess hall, she was dressed in gray regulation knee pants and brown boots. Her short military green jacket was immaculate, the shoulders square, the lapels stiff over olive drab shirt and tie. She was dressed *exactly* as Gray and his companions were dressed. So why did she look so much better? It was amazing what a beautiful woman could do for regulation duds.

But then, Gray was a sucker for a woman in uniform.

She stopped in front of Gray. With her fingers wrapped around his tie, she gave it a sharp yank. She tilted her head and put her mouth close to his. "If you try to fuck me," she said in a low, husky purr, "I'll make *certain* it's the last thing you do."

Gray was forced to laugh, since that's what his friends were doing. The rough sound that burst from his lips was half embarrassment, half male moxie. He locked a fist around her tiny wrist as she started to turn away. "You read minds, Lieutenant? Or just lips?"

"Neither," she responded with a shake of her head. Her long straight hair washed over her slim shoulders as her eyes narrowed on his fist. "Although, if I had my choice, I'd take your lips over your mind. I imagine your mind would be a short read. As for your lips, I have a soft spot for lips like yours." She gave him a sweetly sinful smile. "A very soft, very warm spot."

Gray was momentarily distracted by the idea of her pale legs spread before him, his face buried between her slender thighs, his mouth open against her pussy, his tongue prodding through her damp luscious folds, plucking at her clitoris, delving into her wet opening as she spilled into his mouth. He felt his cock strain against the soft gray fabric that wrapped his hips. The short jacket that barely reached his waist wasn't giving him anything for cover. Gray snorted softly. There was no stopping the hammer once it had made up its mind.

"It was noisy at Etiens," Velvet continued with her explanation. "My ears had to adjust. It was either that or go deaf. Now," she breathed in a sensuous whisper, "there isn't much I don't hear."

"Your ears—" Gray halted. "You're an Adept?"

She smiled silkily as she inclined her chin in answer. "And if you don't hurry up and let go of my wrist, I'm likely to grow poisonous scales."

Gray released her wrist with a jolt, though his keen gaze still smoldered with interest. "You can't adapt that quickly."

She rolled her eyes. "Good call. I love a clever man. Any other questions, Lieutenant?"

"Just one," Gray growled.

She arched one delicate eyebrow in an invitation to proceed.

"When you slit that guy's throat in your dorm, how'd you know your roomie was being attacked? How'd you know she wasn't getting the best fuck of her life?"

"She was screaming," Velvet replied in a slow drawl.

Gray shrugged with casual arrogance. "I thought that was normal."

She blinked once, then shook out her wrist as she turned away. "It was a judgment call," she threw back over her shoulder.

Gray watched her slender hips swing as she sauntered away. Slowly, he lowered himself to the table's bench seat as his wing companions melted down into their seats around him. He nodded resolutely. "I'm gonna fuck that woman," he told his friends in a murmur.

Jason laughed. "Then you'd better hope that her judgment holds out, because when she sees that hammer of yours, she's liable to think you're trying to kill *her*!" Jason shook his head. The overhead light gleamed along the gold strands in his hair. "An Adept! No wonder she has all the male instructors wrapped around her little finger."

"What do you mean?" Matchstick queried, narrowing his bright blue eyes.

"The Adept race can change their physiology to adapt to their environment."

"I know that!" Match shot back. "I know that, given time, they can grow claws or shrink an arm, add an extra lung if they need 'em. But what difference would that make to her instructors?"

Jason rolled his eyes. "Figure it out, Match. She can adjust to accommodate whoever's fucking her. If he's a small man, her cunt will close up for him. If he's a big man, it'll keep getting longer until she can take all of him."

Matchstick's voice was flat. "You're kidding."

Jason shook his head. "An Adept is the perfect fuck. Which means—"

Gray interrupted his friend. "Which means...the hammer has finally found a home."

* * * * *

Twenty minutes later Gray sat slouched at a workstation behind Velvet Meadows. When he'd arrived five minutes late for Advanced Psych, most of the desks were taken. Fortunately for him, the one workstation that was vacant just happened to be behind Lieutenant Meadows' desk at the back of the classroom.

Unfortunately for him, he had a long history with the instructor.

A severe woman with graying hair, Sergeant Watson had glared at him as he'd entered, obviously pissed that he'd arrived late for her first session of Psych. "Lieutenant Hamm," she'd sniped at him, "I see your timing hasn't improved much since your academy days."

He'd offered the older woman a wink and a smile. "I know some women who'd disagree with you, Sergeant Watson." Murmuring laughter had followed Gray down the aisle between the desks as he'd locked his gaze on Velvet. But the elegant little creature had stared straight ahead, her expression serenely disinterested.

Now he sat at the desk behind her, his attention focused on the only woman he'd ever encountered in his entire lifetime who exhibited an utter disinterest in his existence. Gray didn't like being ignored. Not by a woman.

Her hair spilled over her back, one long luxurious curtain of shifting light. Gray sighed contentedly as he imagined the silky skein wrapped up in his fist as he pulled her head back. Her skin was fair—soft and creamy and white—the kind that bruised easily. He couldn't wait to scrape his teeth over her fragile flesh and leave his mark on her throat. Then every other man on the base would know to keep the fuck away from Velvet Meadows. He'd put a hickey on her clit as well. Then Velvet would know who her ass belonged to.

"Mr. Hamm?"

The sergeant's harsh soprano intruded into Gray's daydreams and he glowered at the officer who'd singled him

16

out for attention. Sergeant Watson was obviously waiting for an answer. Scraping his mind back to the topic at hand, Gray weighed his options as he glanced at the clock, hoping that time at least was on his side. It wasn't. Although he'd managed to fantasize his way through forty minutes of class time, he wasn't going to be able to stonewall through the remaining five. The topic was Psychological Warfare. He had no idea what the question was. But when in doubt, the best option was always to agree. "Yes," he answered baldly.

Snickering laughter followed this response as he rolled his shoulder in a defensive gesture. Evidently, he should have gone with no.

"Yes?" the instructor challenged him. "I ask you what kinds of physical stress make a victim most susceptible to brainwashing and you answer...yes?"

Gray felt a light burn etching the high ridge of his cheekbones. He cleared his throat. "I apologize, Sergeant. It's a bad habit. But when a woman asks me a question, it's generally the same question every time—and the answer is almost always yes."

"Really?" The sergeant's eyebrows arched into two sharp peaks as the corner of her mouth twitched wryly. "And on what occasions is the answer no?"

Gray shook his head as he considered his desk with staunch deliberation. "She'd have to be really, really, *really* ugly."

His quick thinking earned him an appreciative round of laughter from his classmates—all except for the young woman seated in front of him. While the rest of his peers chuckled and glanced backward to throw a grin in his direction, Gray could tell Velvet wasn't particularly amused. Her shoulders would have shifted if she'd been laughing.

Her shoulders were as stiff as a damn board.

Now her hand glided up into the air as he watched. The sergeant gave her a nod.

Velvet's voice was cool, liquid silver and cut as neatly as a blade. "While my colleague's answer might be correct on certain occasions, this wasn't one of them. No doubt the lieutenant's brain could do with a good washing...once he manages to drag it out of the gutter. The types of physical stress most conducive to suggestibility are physical trauma, illness and sleep deprivation."

Gray slumped lower in his chair, curling his lip as he sulked. From beneath the dark ridge of his brows, he glowered at Velvet's neat hair and straight shoulders. He wondered how straight-shouldered she'd be in bed. Would she be prim and stiff, or soft and responsive? Would he have to urge her thighs apart with his hands between her legs? Or would she plant her feet and arch beneath him, canting her hips upward to receive his shaft, swallowing his cock whole as she tried to take him hard at the back of her cunt?

Gray pushed out a sigh. So many women, so little time in full gravity.

He ought to be making the most of his time on Earth, wearing out his dick on Bellamy Anders instead of mooning over this arrogant little chit—this arrogant little chit he was going to fuck. After her smart-ass comment, the girl had it coming to her. And pretty soon he'd be giving it to her.

Gray flicked his gaze at the sergeant. At the front of the room, Watson's back was turned as she scrawled with one finger across the static board. Right before him, Velvet's hair hung just beyond the edge of his desk, sleek and tempting. Leaning forward with one large hand, Gray reached slowly for the smooth, silky curtain of sun-washed yellow. His fingers glided through the long strands as he clenched his fist and dragged her head sharply downward.

A soft grunt of surprise was on her full lips as he watched her neck curve backward into a smooth arch. He put his lips close to her ear and breathed in her enigmatic scent. It was clean and sharp. Fresh and cold. Chipped ice and diamonds all the way.

"Just to let you know," he murmured, "the last woman who fucked with me is still licking her wounds."

With the back of her head almost touching Gray's desk, Velvet's expression never flickered. The next thing he saw was her dagger in her small fist, flashing toward his hand. Damn the bitch! She was going to slash his hand open! Gray set his jaw. His fingers tightened in her hair as the blade swished. If there was going to be blood on his desk, the sergeant would know about it. And the old tart would make certain the girl paid.

A second later, Velvet straightened in her seat. She turned to face him as he stared at her, his fist wrapped around the handful of silken sunshine she'd cut from her hair and left in his grasp. "Big deal," she answered coolly. "The last man who fucked *me* is still licking his *cock*."

Gray's jaw dropped.

"*He* couldn't get enough of me." She lifted one delicate shoulder as her eyes shot sparks. "But he got a *whole* lot more than you'll ever get."

Stunned, Gray opened his hand and watched the golden strands spill out over the desk. The lights flicked blue, indicating the class was over. Raising his gaze, he watched Velvet's tight little bottom sway as she strode from the room.

Licking his cock! Gray dropped his hand into his groin, rubbing at the rebellious flesh that surged with a dark, feral hunger. *Licking his cock*! How good would a woman have to taste to have a man licking his cock? Gray frowned as his gaze fell to his groin. And how long would his dick have to be? A jealous growl rumbled in Gray's chest as he collected his computer workpad and slammed out of the classroom.

* * * * *

"And she cut off her hair?" Jason's expression was incredulous.

Gray nodded grimly. "Five inches."

Jason and Gray were crowded into the room that Match shared with the Cajun. Gray slouched in the chair at Matchstick's workstation while Jason occupied the chair opposite him. Match was sitting on the edge of his dorm room bed. The Cajun lay on his back, stretched out on his own narrow cot.

"She's nuts!" Jason snorted. "Didn't she look like an idiot with half her hair missing?"

"It'll grow back," Jed rumbled from his cot. His eyes were closed, his booted feet crossed and propped on the plain plastech footboard at the end of his bed.

"It will—" Jason stopped and banged his palm against his temple. "Of course it will grow back. She's an Adept."

Gray nodded at the floor for several seconds. Finally, he blew out a snort of frustration. "I'm fucking her," he announced.

Jason reached for a small notepad at the corner of the desk and pulled it toward him. "Right. Just tell me where you want your body sent."

Gray shook his head. "I'm gonna be the guy who tames that little hellcat. When I'm done with her, she'll be on her knees, begging…to suck me off."

Jed's voice intruded quietly. "Leave her alone, Hammer. She's been through enough, already."

"Enough already? Are you talking about Etiens? Evidently the blitz was just a day at the beach for Lieutenant Velvet Meadows." Gray nodded resolutely. "I'm fucking her." He lifted one finger to point at his friends. "And you guys are gonna help."

Jed's eyes cracked open into a thin green glare. Reaching behind his head to the shelf above his bed, he picked up a handful of magnetic darts. He gave Gray a malicious look then opened his hand. Three darts lifted from his hand and circled the air above his face, then turned and flew at a picture attached to the side of his workstation.

20

Gray grimaced as the darts smacked into the target.

The target was a picture of him—his groin to be precise. Bellamy Anders had snapped it without his knowledge two years earlier as he'd approached her with his cock in his fist. Being a materials expert, the little witch had coated the hammer with a magnetic attraction field.

The darts homed in on the tip of his erection and exploded into three spurting showers of thin paper streamers, the suggestion being that Gray was whacking off.

Women were evil.

And Spaceforce women were *damn* evil.

Gray smiled. That didn't stop him from wanting to fuck every last one of them. And as far as practical jokes were concerned, Bellamy's exploding dick was pretty clever.

Matchstick's lopsided smile was pure mischief. "Why should we help? What's in it for us?"

As Gray watched the thin streamers flutter down toward Jed's boots, he came to a quick decision. "What's in it for you? You guys get to watch me fuck the ass off Little Miss Chipped Ice and Diamonds. Matchstick, can you lift the filmcam out of my workpad and turn it into a remote eye?"

A grin crept over the redhead's mouth, widening as it grew. "I can do better than that. I can put an eye on the end of your dick."

Gray laughed. "Which won't hurt your view one bit."

"Not one bit. Just give us a good shot of her pussy before you go in for the kill."

"Okay," Gray continued with businesslike malice, "can you make the filmcam stick to a metal desk?"

"No problem," Match replied with enthusiasm. "I'll rob some electrons from the copper film. It will stick like glue."

"Good. Jason, can you get the codes that will allow you to initiate a short burst from the invasion alarm?"

"Real or drill?"

"Real. Make it a two-second burst, so it'll look like a false alarm. Command will just shrug it off as a static buildup in the hardware. We *don't* want to get Command pissed." Gray turned to Jed, sprawled out on his bunk. "Cajun, can you get us access to—"

But Jed cut him off. "Leave me outta this," he growled. "Meadows is your problem, not mine. Besides, I have Advanced Weapons with her. I don't wanna get my head blown off...just so you can get yours *sucked* off."

Gray frowned suspiciously as his eyes narrowed on Jed. That was a long speech for the Cajun. First he'd warned Gray to leave Velvet alone. Now he was refusing to help. Gray shot a quizzical look at Jason but his best friend just shrugged.

If Jason was his best friend, Lieutenant Jed Castille had to be his best rival. Graduating from the space academy at the top of their class, the two men were constantly on the lookout to outdo one another. Since they were so evenly matched in the classroom as well as in flight, they continued their battle outside on the *playing* field, vying for the attention of the opposite sex.

Currently, Gray was ahead.

But when it came to the ladies, Jed was a formidable foe. With that thick, unruly brown hair, dark coloring and remarkably pale green eyes, Jed attracted more than his fair share of attention. His cold, withdrawn personality only served to intrigue the ambitious young women of the Force. Female officers were always looking for a challenge when it came to men, always looking for a bad boy. And Jed had to be the ultimate bad boy. He shrugged most women off with disinterest—which was probably why Gray was currently ahead.

Gray wasn't disinterested in women. Not by a long shot.

Gray couldn't even pretend to be disinterested.

It had taken several combat runs before Gray and Jed had finally learned to work together. With direct precision, Jed supplied the team with information, scenarios, alternatives. As wing leader, Gray made the decisions. Matchstick was the systems expert, though Jed was no slouch when it came to electromechanics or materials for that matter. Jason was the team's software polisher.

Matchstick's snort interrupted Gray's musing. "I think the Cajun likes her," he taunted.

Jed turned his liquid green gaze on the redhead. "Fuck you," he murmured on a yawn.

"The Cajun had better *not* like her," Gray growled. "You hear that, Jed? I don't want you screwing this up."

"Screw this up? Me?" Jed's eyes were closed again. "You don't need my help to screw this up, Gray. You can do that all by yourself."

Chapter Two

ಬ

Approximately four minutes after the alarms sounded at midnight, Gray stood outside the door to Velvet's dorm room. Dressed in soft gray regulation knee pants and high boots, he reached a hand into his groin, hefting his cock into his cupped palm as he rubbed a thumb over the tiny eye he'd applied to the top of his dick. About the size of a small freckle, the camera eye was inconspicuous enough that the girl would never see it, unless she went looking for it.

He'd just have to make sure she didn't go looking for it. That was okay. He wasn't planning on fucking her mouth. It was her hot, sweet little pussy that Gray hungered for. He longed for the heat of her wet cunt kissing his dick as she bucked against him and came on his cock.

Conquest.

That's what this was all about.

Women weren't like men. Generally, they weren't distracted by men as sex objects. A woman didn't see a man and automatically imagine him naked, or wonder how good he was in bed. Her eyes didn't automatically gravitate to his cock, the way a man's would home in on a woman's tits or pussy. Women were so fucking cool and independent. It took so much damn work to get their barriers down and get them into bed. Gray smiled. But when you *did* finally get a woman spread out beneath you, it didn't take long before the ice thawed and the independence cracked. Once you got between her legs, it was only a matter of time before a woman broke down, whimpering and moaning and sobbing, absolutely defeated in her need for completion. He usually gave a woman several orgasms before he took his own release. It wasn't an

24

act of generosity. He did it for himself, reveling in the gritty satisfaction that accompanied his partner's total submission.

Conquest was the goal. Sex and conquest and delicious whimpering women, sobbing out your name as you fucked their warm, wet slits.

With that thought in mind, Gray reached inside his jacket, pulling from an interior pocket the larger camera that Matchstick had prepared. With the thin copper filmboard hidden inside his palm, Gray tugged down on his short green jacket. He straightened his tie. Having run out of any further adjustments that would delay his next act, he took a breath and lifted his loosely closed fist. With his knuckles, Gray gave the wooden door a light rap.

Velvet answered the door and immediately stepped back. Her amethyst eyes were wide but calm as she gazed at him. Her slim arms were crossed over the standard classroom notebook she hugged to her chest. The notebook's once-yellow cover was stained and battered, the edges bruised, the pages thick at the corners.

Since Gray's team had timed the short alarm for the middle of the night, she was wearing the clothes she slept in—a soft T-shirt that barely covered her prim little ass. The fabric fell softly around her graceful curves, clinging to the sides of her pert, round breasts.

"Hi," he murmured in a low voice already roughened with lust. "I just thought I'd check on you. You okay?"

She took another step backward, smiling uncertainly as she lifted one shoulder. "It was probably just a false alarm."

He nodded, driving her ahead of him as he forged into the room. With nowhere to go, she backed up and lowered herself to the narrow, single bed she slept in. The door swung silently to close behind him.

"Yeah," he agreed with a soft laugh. "Static buildup," he offered.

"It was nice of you to check on me," she murmured politely, her eyes flicking to the door, which was probably his cue to turn around and use it. But Gray wasn't going anywhere.

He pushed a hand back through his hair. "My room is just a few doors down," he explained with a friendly smile. Pretending nonchalance, he leaned against the corner of her workstation, sliding his hand down the side of the desk and pressing the thin slice of copper filmboard against the black metal. The slight negative charge sucked the camera from his hand. It stuck to the desk, just as Matchstick had promised.

"I wanted to make sure you were okay," he said ingratiatingly. "And I was curious about your hair," he added, improvising on the spot.

Hugging her notebook closer in one arm, she turned her head and combed her fingers through the ragged ends of her hair. The edges of her lips curled into a tentative smile. "It's growing back."

He chuckled. "I thought you were going to take my fingers off."

She tilted her head. "I considered it." She lowered her gaze to the floor then lifted it again, catching him in the spellbinding color of her eyes. "You didn't flinch."

Held captive by her gaze, Gray's breath hitched in his throat. Admiration shone in her eyes. Deep, royal purple admiration. He was right. She was the sort of woman who spoke whole sentences with her eyes. He shifted his weight as an inconvenient surge of guilt nipped sharply at the edges of his resolve. Shaking it off, he crossed his brawny arms over his chest as he smiled down at her.

"My name's Gray, by the way. Graham Hamm."

She dipped her head in acknowledgment. "I've heard about you, your friends and *your* nickname."

He faked a wincing grimace. "Don't let any of that scare you off."

26

She lifted one slim shoulder. "I don't scare easily."

Gray nodded. That much was obvious. "What do you have there?" he asked softly.

"This?" She tucked the notebook more tightly against her chest. "Just some drawings."

He extended his hand toward her, palm up. "May I see?"

She hesitated an instant before she handed the book up to him.

Turning in the narrow space between the desk and the bed, Gray used the book as an excuse to sit down beside her, intensely aware of her as he thumbed through the worn pages. "These are good," he murmured, slowing down to take a closer look at her pencil sketches.

Her drawings *were* good. Not polished but very earthy and…alive. All the sketches depicted young men and women, vibrant with energy. Eyes sparkling, eyebrows arched, lips curled into dimpled cheeks. "Your style is unique," he murmured. He pulled a thick finger along the edge of a young man's blowing hair. "All these little lines give the subject action, movement."

"I didn't have an eraser," she explained softly.

"Were these live subjects?" he asked her.

When she didn't answer, he checked her face. Her dark eyes were wide as she gazed up at him. *Jeezis.* Something was wrong. The girl looked like someone had just ripped her heart out.

Confused, Gray frowned as he rephrased the question. "Were they live models?"

Slowly, she shook her head. "I did them from memory," she said in an unsteady contralto.

Gray's stomach dropped with a sick, hollow thud. A hard lump lodged in his throat, just above his Adam's apple. "From memory?"

27

"Yeah," she answered, her voice barely audible. "I did them at Etiens."

Jeezis. It was her notebook from the bunker. The one she'd gone back for after the rescue team had arrived.

Uncertain as to how to proceed, he flipped through the pages slowly, silently buying time. "This was your unit," he said quietly and felt her shift beside him as she nodded. He turned the book sideways to view the next page. "This one's recent, isn't it? She's a pretty girl," he told her, hoping it was the right thing to say. Gray had two years in Weapons Training and three semesters in Psych Warfare...and not one single credit to his name when it came to Grief Management.

Her arm pressed against his side as she leaned into him. "My sister. She's in repo."

"Oh shit," he muttered. He dropped the notebook, wrapping an arm around her as he pulled her into his chest. "Shit, I'm sorry, Velvet."

He held her small tense body against his, lust and tenderness warring in his soul, tearing at his heart. While he was swamped with an inherent male instinct to protect the slender slip of a woman caught in his embrace, an equally primal and urgent need ripped through his blood and thickened his cock in hard, driving surges.

She caught at a series of small, dry sobs and he squeezed her tighter, as though if he clasped her tightly enough, he could stop her from crying and end her sorrow. After a long tense moment, she finally took a breath. "I've never shown them to anyone," she said into his chest. Her voice was calmly stoic. "They were...like family. After Etiens, after losing...everything, I've been a little reluctant about getting close to anyone."

With the top of her head tucked under his chin, Gray shook his head. She spent her free time alone in her room with what was left of her family—the drawings in this book, her memories, keeping her friends alive in the only way she could.

The coldness she projected was a shield devised to protect her heart from future loss. Her murderous agility a tool she'd honed in order to survive.

But she wasn't cold as he held her in his arms. She was warm and small and vulnerable. And the lust which had accompanied him into her room was now something far more powerful and greatly more frightening. Lightly, he ran his fingers into her hair, tangling them in the pale silken strands as he thumbed her cheekbones. Her eyelids were at half-mast, her gaze locked on his lips.

He gave them to her. He gave her his lips. The circumstances called for a long, tender, loving kiss and that's what he gave her. He gave her everything. And when she pressed her round, firm breasts into his chest, he reached for them as automatically as breathing.

Normally when he kissed a woman, it was a ruthless act of dominance as well as an insistent demand for more—a demand for hot liquid sex and a hard fuck. This was different. This was so mind-shatteringly different he couldn't tell up from down, despite the presence of gravity.

He just knew he couldn't stop kissing her.

Maybe it was because he was giving for once in his life instead of taking.

Normally Gray controlled the situation when it came to women and sex, manipulating the woman in careful degrees through each step that would lead him to conquest—the hand on the knee, the palm on the breast, the fingers between the legs, slipping inside her clothing, unfastening her bra, working his way inside her panties—each step executed with precise art, with one goal in mind as his partner gradually yielded up everything to his advance.

A finger between the hot lips of her sex. Then his cock nudging at her opening. Fucking her while she wrapped her legs around his hips and screamed. Pulling his wet cock from her pussy and fucking her mouth while she was still drowsy with pleasure. Pulling out and painting her lips with a sheen of pre-cum then spreading her sex open with his fingers, working her clit with the flat of his tongue until she was ready to go again. Turning her roughly as he eased into her from behind, sinking deep, his balls swinging against her wet sex as he fingered her clit and fucked her into another orgasm before he finally came inside her dark, tight, clenching channel.

That was control. This wasn't. This was just searing, burning, scathing, mindless need. Gasping for breath, he twisted his lips on hers, tangled up in so much emotion he thought his heart would shatter and explode. He murmured her name as his large palm slid over the perfection of her small plump breast. His hand kept covering the same ground, as though he couldn't get enough of her, as though he was trying to tell her with that one hand on her breast how much he needed her.

Without knowing how he got there, he found himself stretched out on top of her, his hand inside the soft white T-shirt that was pushed up over her precious tits. Together they moved on the bed, her body undulating beneath his in feminine waves of passion, rolling beneath him as though he was already inside her, as though she was riding his cock. He was still fully clothed. And he was still kissing her as though his life depended on it. It was the most intensely intimate moment he'd ever shared with a woman. And whatever it was he was experiencing, they were definitely sharing it. She appeared to be as lost to passion as was he.

Somewhere deep in his psyche, a small silent word tugged at his conscience.

Camera.

He wanted to stop. His mind told him he *had* to stop. Somewhere in his tortured consciousness, buried deep beneath a thick layer of smothering lust, someone was screaming, "*Abort, Abort, Abort.*" Strangely enough, they were screaming it in his voice. But his cock was emitting so much fucking static, the message just wasn't getting through. Gray crushed

Velvet's body beneath his as his hips kept grinding her into the hard mattress. Beneath his mouth, she was making small sobbing sounds of distress, the needy little noises urging him on. He groaned as he ground the thick ridge of his cock into her flat belly. He could feel her nipples, tight, hard and excited, pressing against his palm. He wanted—he needed—to get his mouth on her tits and kiss the daring little nubs that strained beneath his palm.

The camera!

Abort! Abort! Abort!

Gray gasped as he broke the kiss. He stared down at his fingers curled around the soft fabric he'd wadded up over her nipples, baring her breast to the camera. Fuck! He had to stop. He had to leave.

He had to fuck her—now.

Drawing in a breath rough with overpowering hunger, he tugged Velvet's shirt down to cover her breasts as she writhed beneath him. He was absolutely, definitely going to leave. Right now!

Her hands snaked upward and wrapped around his neck. With her fingers knotted in his hair, she thrust her breasts into his chest and pulled his mouth back down onto hers. He groaned again as she fed her breath into his mouth. Her taste was incredible. Hot and clean. Intoxicating, like the best sparkling vodka burning on ice.

He had to do something. Damage Control!

"Velvet," he rasped. "Velvet, we have to move."

When he pulled her to her feet, she staggered a bit. Her hands were beneath the hem of her T-shirt, her fingers working feverishly, pushing her panties down over the shallow curve of her hips, baring her pussy for him.

Moving swiftly to shield her from the camera, Gray picked her up and shoved her at the door, out of the camera's visual range. With his fingers hooked beneath her ass, he pulled her upward until her face was level with his then pinned her beneath his body, plastered against the door, while he worked on the presslock that closed his knee pants. His fingers were shaking as he shoved his cock pocket out of the way and guided his dick out with his hand. With a deep, shuddering sigh, he slid the wide, rounded head through her burning folds.

"Fuck!" he cursed. The eye! The remote eye was sucking at the head of his dick like an evil leech. "Fuck!" he wrenched out, using his short, blunt fingernails to tear the sticky eye from the tightly stretched flesh that rounded his cock head. Dropping the tiny disk to the floor, he crunched the tiny camera under the heel of his boot.

Her head tipped backward and a look of ecstasy fell over her face as he fed his cock through her damp folds. "Are...are you covered?" she breathed out in a soft rush of words.

"Yes," he panted back.

"I didn't see you take anything."

"I just pop one every morning," he grunted, "in case I get lucky."

"I-Isn't that a waste?" she mumbled.

For a moment he stared at her. At this point, his brain was firing on one cylinder. Why was she asking so many questions? He could hardly think, let alone put together enough words to form any sort of an answer. Her lips were parted, a luscious pale pink. Her gaze was sultry, her eyes downcast as she watched his mouth. "I usually get lucky," he rasped back at her.

She tilted her head forward and brushed her mouth against his chin.

Gray groaned as her lips dampened the stubble at the edge of his jaw. Her moist heat, dragging along his jawline, whetted his need into sharp, urgent, driving intensity. With his shaft in his hand, he slid his cock head back through her slot until he found her deep, soft notch. Flexing his knees, he fed her his fat tip. He gasped as the tight kiss of her pussy closed around his first few inches. He stopped, taking in quick shallow breaths, on the edge of losing everything right there at the beginning.

She wrapped her long, slender legs around his hips. "I'll be small this time," she murmured in adorable apology, "but I'll adjust after a while. Eventually I'll be able to take all of you."

He groaned again, this time in absolute agony. Her words were being transmitted to the workstation in his dormitory, where his friends were listening to every panted word, every muted sigh, every compromising confession she uttered. "Shhh," he urged her. "Shhh, little one. Don't say a word."

He slid his hands beneath her soft, stretchy shirt and forged upward. Finally he had those sweet round tits in his hands again. With his fingers curled to cup the sides of her breasts, he thumbed the dainty pink nubs at the center of her areolas. His hips strained upward as he straightened his knees and tried to force his cock into her impossibly small channel. "Jeezis Skies, you're tight," he whispered. "Relax, sweetheart. Try to take me in."

In agonizing increments, he worked his cock into her slim little sheath, a sweat breaking out across his skin as he forged his way inside her. When he'd gone as far as her body would allow, he tried a few slow thrusts. Her inner walls held him like a burning fist, dragging on the hungry flesh that strained over his erection, squeezing his shaft like there was no tomorrow. A new wash of wet heat coated his cock on the third thrust—she was creaming for him already.

He moaned when she gasped in pleasure. She was so ready. And he was so ready to give it to her.

Reaching behind him, Gray unwrapped her legs and hooked them beneath his forearms. With his hands below her knees and pulling her wide, he spread her against the door as he hammered into her. The room thrummed to a pounding erotic rhythm blending into a delicious carnal symphony—the dull thud of Velvet's backside being driven into the wooden door, the harsh slap of hard male muscle smacking against damp feminine flesh, the small murmuring noises coming from her lips, the sound of his own deep grunts mixed with rough masculine sobs.

Velvet's breath caressed his cheek in soft whimpering pants and small helpless murmurs. His cock thickened at the sounds of her surrender while he groaned, torn between heaven and hell. The alpha male in him wanted to hear the girl cry out as he fucked her. The gentleman in him wanted to shut the lady up before she compromised herself any further in front of his eavesdropping friends. Inconveniently for Gray, his alpha male side was headquartered in his dick and it was doing most of the talking.

The gentleman in him growled, fighting its way to the surface. Covering her lips with his, Gray silenced her with his mouth. The belated action was half sheltering protection— shielding her from the listening ears of his friends. The other half was just plain selfishness. He didn't want to share this with anyone. He wanted all of this. He wanted this for himself alone.

With his mouth pressed against hers, he muffled her cries as she started to come. Her arms slipped inside his and her fingernails bit into his ass as she pulled him into her, demanding cock—all of it and now! Her mouth slipped from beneath his as she bucked under his weight, her wet mouth sliding along his jawline, her teeth nipping sharply at his earlobe. Gray jerked at the slight bite of pain, his cock slamming to the back of her vagina. Reclaiming her lips, he grunted a shuddering moan into her mouth, straining against her a long, final time as he experienced several seconds of pure, perfect bliss. His cock surged in a final delicious expansion, the pressure and heat and wet, wet pleasure surrounding his dick as her cunt crushed down on his shaft and his ejaculation surged and shot from his dick like a fucking flamethrower.

This was it. This was absolute nirvana. His thick seed squeezed down the sides of his shaft, bathing his cock and filling her sheath as it joined them together in a perfect, dark union of intimacy.

When he came out of orgasm, his chest was heaving, his sex-damp body sealed against hers, his cheek wet where it touched her temple. Her tears didn't surprise him half as much as his own. His forehead fell against the door as he sucked at the air, his eyes burning as he tried to work his way through the mess of emotions dicking with his head.

There was a lot of sympathy in there along with tenderness and sorrow. A gut-wrenching ache he couldn't put a name to. A bare, bald instinct to protect and claim. To possess no matter what the cost, to dominate if necessary. Mixed up with all of that was a sharp sense of self-recrimination. Velvet had been through so much. He might have considered that before he'd set out to bring her to her knees. He'd known her history. But instead of giving her the benefit of any doubt whatsoever, he'd misjudged her completely. He'd come to her room planning to knock the proud girl off her pedestal. He'd succeeded so fucking completely that he could almost feel the shards of her cool reserve stabbing him through the heart.

He checked her face as she lifted her eyes to his. Her expression made his throat tighten into a painful knot. Her quiet gaze was tender and thankful. He'd fucked her up against a door and the girl was thankful!

He was a dick. No doubt about it.

With a shudder of defeat, he turned his face and put his lips against the smooth, heated flesh at the base of her throat. "I'm sorry," he murmured as he lapped at her flesh with his rough tongue, preparing her skin for his mark. "I'm sorry," he whispered before he sucked her flesh between his teeth. He sucked and soothed and lapped, abrading her flesh with his tongue, scraping the smooth satin between his teeth. Finally, he pulled back to observe his work — the small bruise blushing prettily on the creamy backdrop of her pale skin. He pulled in a long shuddering breath and branded her mouth with a hard kiss and a primitive growl of dominance, letting her know in no uncertain terms that *she* was his.

From this point onward, Velvet Meadows belonged to the Hammer.

* * * * *

Less than an hour later, Gray opened the door to the room he shared with Jason. Relief washed over his tight nerve endings as he gazed into the mercifully dark room. Through some chance miracle, his friends weren't crowded around his workpad — grinning and congratulating him on his victory.

Stumbling toward his workstation, Gray groped around in the gloom, locating his computer by touch. With the wafer-thin workpad clenched between his thumb and forefinger, he pulled back his elbow and snapped his wrist. His computer hit the wall with a harsh smack. He kept smashing it against the wall until it split and fell into thin bits of black plastech and brightly colored filmboard. When he was sure it was dead, he flung the shattered remnants at the wastebasket beneath his desk. With that out of the way, he dropped onto the hard surface of his bed, stomach churning with an unfamiliar emotion — self-loathing.

At least he *assumed* that's what was making him feel sick. He'd just done something wrong. That didn't happen often. Gray was usually right. Quick, fast, clever and almost always right. With his elbows on his knees, Gray cradled his head in his hands, ignoring his roommate's soft curse. "Did I wake you?" he growled.

"No," Jason answered. "It wasn't you. It was the asteroid that just plowed into the dormitory."

Gray rubbed his hands over his eyes. "That wasn't an asteroid — just an ass."

Jason's voice was cautious. "Are you all right?" he asked, continuing swiftly when Gray didn't answer. "We didn't watch, Gray. We turned the workpad off when we realized what was going on, when you dropped her notebook."

"Thanks," he muttered on a hopeless sigh, shaking his head at the floor.

"Are you okay?" Jason asked again.

"We've got to get that camera out of there."

Jason switched on the lamp that hung over his bed. The faint glow of light fell over his startled expression. "It's still in her room? Why—why didn't you bring it out with you?"

Gray groaned. "I couldn't get it off the desk! Damn Matchstick anyway!"

Jason looked worried as he levered himself into a sitting position. "Well, you asked him to make it stick."

Gray snorted with frustration. "For the first time in my life, I wished I had fingernails. *Long* fingernails!"

"Couldn't you get your dagger—"

"Not without her noticing!" Gray shouted back at his best friend.

Jason flinched as his gaze turned defensive.

Immediately, Gray regretted his outburst. Jason had had enough crap land on him in his lifetime without Gray adding to it. The white scar that ripped down the left side of his roommate's face wasn't as deep as the scars he kept hidden within. "I'm sorry, Jase."

"No. It's all right," he muttered, pushing his blond hair out of his eyes. "But why didn't you stay longer? Spend the night with her? You could have pried it off when she showered in the morning!"

"The dorm super kicked me out of her room," he groaned. "We were making too much noise!"

"Fuck," Jason whispered, his voice quiet with awe.

"We have to get back into her room," Gray said, strategizing as he spoke. "Wake up the Cajun. He's going to have to help."

Jason reached for his communicator on the shelf above his bed. With one hand, he slipped the long copper curl onto the shell of his ear. His hazel eyes connected with Gray's before he spoke to the communicator, "Ring the Cajun."

* * * * *

Jed was awake when Jason's call came in on his communicator. He was sitting at his workstation, hooked up to the Universal Library and reading...about Adepts. The room was quiet. Matchstick had found somewhere else to spend the night. Either that or he was still in Jason's room, watching Gray with Velvet.

Jed had been intrigued by Velvet's comments about her hearing. He'd been watching her before the Hammer even entered the mess hall earlier that morning. He'd glimpsed her from behind his half-closed eyes and couldn't—*could not*—take his eyes off her.

It wasn't just that she was beautiful. Or even that she was his ideal when it came to women. Unlike most of his comrades, the Cajun was attracted to small women with slender frames and girlish figures. His mouth watered just thinking about her stripped and naked, her small plump tits, her demure little ass. But there was something more where Velvet was concerned. She had some indefinable quality that called to him. Something that made him want to make her smile. Something that made him want to protect her.

Jed snorted. He was hardly Galahad material and there were a number of women who'd back him up on that point.

Besides, from all appearances, the young officer didn't need protecting. She'd survived Etiens. And she'd sure as hell put the Hammer in his place, there in the mess hall. She was, after all, a Spaceforce lieutenant. As such, she would be a highly trained combatant as well as a competent tactician. And he'd seen her in Advanced Weapons! The babe was a beast when she got a blastuka in her hands.

He'd concentrated on her hearing since he didn't want to think about her, his reaction to her or the fact that the Hammer was probably fucking her at that very moment.

Jed pushed out a tense sigh as he pulled his workpad toward him.

It was hard to imagine how the ear-splitting barrage at Etiens could have enhanced Velvet's hearing, instead of rendering her deaf. He understood how, as an Adept, her hearing could have adapted to close out *all* sound but how could it have adjusted to pick up whispered words from across a room at the same time?

As he continued his research, Jed learned that it would be hard to predict how an Adept would adjust to any given situation. Small variations in conditions could bring about unexpected adaptations. But he found and read about a similar case where an Adept musician had been known to simultaneously tune out any noise above eighty decibels while amplifying everything below five. Jed leaned back in his chair, rubbing his eyes.

That seemed to be a reasonable representation of what had happened to Velvet's hearing. The question remained…what had happened to her mind? As far as he was concerned, she shouldn't have one anymore. How had she adapted to handle the stress and fear, the deprivation and the emotional assault of being trapped in a tiny bunker for ninety days, bombarded by polyrounds, watching as most of her unit died around her, wondering if the next polyround would have her name on it?

Opening another drive on his workpad, Jed accessed the Base security recordings, trying out several variations on old cheats before he got past the firewall and into the visual documents. Once inside the mess hall visuals, he sped backward through the time file. He stopped the document then let it play forward again, zooming in on Velvet sitting alone at her table.

He slid his hand into his groin without thinking, palming the presslock on his knee pants as he watched the visual playback of Velvet. She reminded him of a porcelain doll. Every feature carefully composed. As quiet and still as an eYonan morning. He zoomed in on her face, watching her eyes carefully for the next ten minutes as he stroked his dick. Her eyes were as quiet as her face...until Gray walked in. For a brief instant, he caught a flicker of interest in the shadowed depths of her gaze.

A muscle ticced in his jaw as he clenched his teeth. She'd never glanced in Jed's direction. He'd known for certain that was the case because he'd been watching her the whole time. She'd never turned her gaze his way. He didn't like the fact that it was Gray who'd captured her interest. If she'd seen him first, maybe her eyes would have come alive for an instant, as they had for Gray. And though he hated to admit it—even to himself—Jed had a feeling there was more than pure rivalry involved in his reaction.

He closed the file, disgusted with himself, disgusted with her but mostly disgusted with the Hammer. With one finger, he opened the presslock on his pants and dug his shaft out of his cock pocket. Like a dark snake, it sprang taut and hard against his flat belly.

He thumbed the wide crown a few times then wrapped his fingers around his shaft and started pumping slowly. Velvet's features flashed through his mind as he stroked his cock—her small fey face, her pointed chin, her wide, soft mouth. The little Adept had his cock in a twist. His fist bit down hard, nearly bruising his shaft, the veins on the back of his hand bulging as it shook with tension. His other hand joined his first and the fingers of both tightened around his cock then loosened a hairsbreadth. He flexed his hips and fed his shaft through his cased fingers. His cock pulsed and throbbed and burned with a sharp urgency as he drove it between his hands.

Fuck! Just thinking about her turned his balls to bricks of steel.

When he was close to ejaculation, he opened his hands suddenly, panting as he watched his cock twitch against his belly, staring at his pre-cum coating the head of his dick. Longingly, he thought about Velvet's mouth. Her shy tongue curling around his swollen cock head, licking away that sheen of hot moisture. He closed his eyes and imagined guiding her down to her knees as he stood over her, offering her everything Gray could give her and more, holding her chin in his palm and swabbing the wet crown of his cock over her mouth, gliding a hand down his shaft and coming on her mouth, painting her lips with his cum.

With his semen glossing her lips, he'd drop to his knees and kiss her, licking his cum from her mouth and pulling her into his arms, reaching for her pussy, exploring her slit carefully, learning her secrets in intimate detail, fingering her folds and finding her clit then pleasuring her over and over again until her moisture ran over his hands and he was hard again.

"Fuck," he groaned, levering himself suddenly from his chair and staggering to the small bathroom at the end of the room. He reached the sink just in time to come into the stainless steel bowl, bracing himself with one hand on the mirror in front of him, stroking his cock with the other, watching with slitted eyes as he erupted from the slit on his cock head and coated the shallow bowl with his milky ejaculate. "Jeezis." He mangled the curse between his gritted teeth. He fisted his hand against the mirror, pounding the glass as he came in long surges. "By the Princess. Fuck!"

After the last rush of release had flashed up the length of his shaft, he dropped his hands to the counter. His chin drooped onto his chest, and he stared at the cum he'd spewed into the sink's bowl.

41

He shook his head. Something had him riding a hard edge of need. He just wasn't ready to admit *who* that something was.

After rinsing his cum down the drain, Jed tucked his dick back into his cock pocket and washed his hands. Pulling his hands back through his rowdy locks, he returned to his workstation. That's when the call came in from Jason. He rubbed his eyes. It was two o'clock in the morning.

Just as he'd predicted, Gray had fucked himself over.

Chapter Three

℅

Gray pushed the scrambled eggs around on his plate. Some things never changed. Usually, they were the things that didn't need improving—like breakfast.

Despite the introduction of exotic delicacies from across the universe, eggs and bacon prevailed as a popular favorite at Earth Base Ten. The hearty breakfast aromas of fresh coffee, fried potatoes and crisp bacon, golden eggs and brown toast would normally have had Gray's stomach growling—this morning it was just churning.

"Here he comes," Jason alerted Gray.

Gray jumped to his feet and strode across the mess hall to meet the Cajun. Jed was a genius when it came to getting past mechanical door locks. And Gray was counting on Jed to save his ass. "Did you get the camera?"

Jed shook his head.

Gray almost exploded as he trailed Jed back toward the table where he'd left Jason and Match. "What the fuck! Did you get into her room?"

"It wasn't there," Jed intoned calmly.

"What do you mean, it wasn't there?" Grabbing Jed by the shoulder, Gray spun him around. "Don't fuck with me, Cajun."

Jed shoved him off, his eyes glowering green slits. "I got her door open, got into her room. The camera wasn't there. *She* wasn't there. End of story."

Gray fisted his hands in the lapels of Jed's short, green jacket. "It had to be there!" He halted, suddenly suspicious. "You didn't...tell her about it."

43

Jed snorted as he shook his head. "Get a grip, man. I wouldn't do that."

"Yeah, *right*. Like you'd care what she thought of me."

Shaking his head, Jed pushed out an unkind laugh. "When I agreed to help, I didn't do it for you, Hammer. I did it for her."

"What do you mean?"

Jed slid onto the bench seat as he gave Gray a condescending look of disgust. "I didn't want to see her get hurt."

Gray dropped onto the seat beside the Cajun. He felt blank. He felt sick. The camera wasn't there. She must have found it. "I'm fucked," he moaned out on a snarl, scraping his hands back through his thick brush of hair.

When Jed failed to follow this up with any sort of snide remark, Gray lifted his face suspiciously. A cold shiver of foreboding chased up his spine and a still silence settled over the table as he stared at Jed. Slowly, Gray shifted his eyes and followed Jed's gaze across the mess hall.

It was Velvet.

Gray stood as she approached the table at a slow saunter. His heart was hammering hard enough to drive nails. She was wearing her regulation knee pants—just like his, only about ten sizes smaller. The soft gray wool blend hugged her hips and tucked into her boots. Her tie was missing and the top three buttons of her dress shirt were undone, showing a lot of skin in the open neckline. The rumpled olive shirt was pulled tight across her round breasts. Her cheeks were flushed pink, her uneven hair hanging in wisps around her delicate face. She looked like she'd just rolled out of bed...after being rolled *in* bed.

Which was just about the case.

Gray groaned at the sight of her lips, bruised and swollen, a beaten shade of dark rose. At the base of her neck, off to one side, was the small bruise he'd left on her skin. Now that she was on display, out in the middle of the officers' mess hall, Gray itched to button up her collar and cover her, to hide the long line of her pale throat, the soft swell of her round breasts—to tie her to the end of his bed and hide her from the sight of all other men. She was the most beautiful thing he'd ever seen.

And she was angry.

She was angry, all right. Pissed as hell. Although her face didn't show it, Velvet radiated a bright, vicious energy as she strode toward him. When she reached their table, she turned her small hand palm up. Gray caught a glimmer of bright copper just before she slammed the filmcam down on the table.

"You're good," she told him with clipped indifference. "You'd make a damn good double agent. If you ever want to apply for a position with Counter Esp, let me know. I'll give you a reference." Planting both palms on the table, she leaned forward to give his three companions a perfect view inside her open shirt. Her luscious breasts nestled together cozily inside her low-cut bra. "Hope your friends enjoyed the show," she drawled.

"Velvet," he stammered. "I'm sorry. It's…it's not as bad as you think."

She shrugged as she swung her hips and sauntered away. "I'm an Adept. I'll adjust. As a matter of fact, I'm growing claws right now. Next time you come around, they should be long enough to rip your heart out."

Gray winced. A murmured sound of agony made its way past his lips. Even to his own ears, it sounded as though his heart was breaking. "Velvet!" he shouted. Following her, Gray reached for her elbow to turn her around.

She turned on him swiftly. Her long, slim, razor-sharp dagger was in her hand, its deadly tip pressed tightly beneath the jutting line of his jaw, the same jaw she'd favored only hours ago with the soft press of her lips. "Thank me," she hissed. "Thank me now, you Class One prick."

Her fist moved a fraction of an inch and Gray felt the cold bite of metal against his skin, followed by a warm trickle of blood. "What am I thanking you for?" he rasped from a tight throat.

Her voice was a quiet slice of sound. "For not shoving that camera up your ass where it belongs."

He felt the blade cut deeper, felt the trickle of blood turn into a stream, felt his collar warming as the fabric sucked up his blood. "I'm sorry," he said quietly.

In one smooth motion, she sheathed her dagger and turned on her heel.

Gray watched her stalk away, his cheeks on fire. As she strode through the mess hall doors, he turned to face his friends.

Jason tried to give him a smile. "That could have been worse."

"Only if she'd killed me," Gray muttered, pressing his thumb over the small wound at the top of his neck.

There was a scrape of sound as Jed's boots cleared the bench seat and hit the floor. "If you gentlemen will excuse me," he announced, straightening this tie, "I have a beautiful woman to catch." With those words and a malicious backward glance at Gray, Jed followed Velvet across the hall, through the doors and out into the sunlit yard.

Gray watched Jed's back, panic boiling up inside him as he snarled out the filthiest obscenity he could put on his lips — followed by the word "traitor".

Jed and he had always been rivals. But the stakes had never been so high. Their friendship was on the line this time. Gray stormed across the hall, almost tripping over a busboy 'droid before he slammed out into the sunlit yard. Growling all the way, he cut a straight line across the manicured lawn, taking the shortest route possible to where Velvet stood with

Made For Two Rivals

Jed. The Cajun had his hand on her elbow. Gray planned to correct that situation. Gray intended to remove Jed's hand— from his arm if necessary.

Coming up behind his two fellow officers, Gray grabbed Jed by the collar of his jacket and spun him around.

Jed's eyes held a quiet warning. "Alpha Tango," he cut at Gray.

Gray hesitated an instant before military discipline kicked in. There were some things you just didn't question. Alpha Tango was one of them. It was a command to shut up and listen. The information that followed those two words had saved his life more than once in his brief but challenging military career.

With a vicious growl, he gave Jed a separating shove.

The Cajun stumbled back a few steps then maneuvered himself in front of Velvet. Gray's growl deepened as Jed faced Velvet and placed his hands on her hips. But Jed's piercing green gaze never left his. "Come closer," Jed told him.

Gray tensed. Something was wrong. He might be pissed as hell at Jed right now—easily as pissed as he'd ever been in his lifetime. But something was going on. He could see it in Jed's eyes. Something important. Something that had nothing to do with the woman he was holding. Gray scanned the yard, looking for trouble. "What's wrong?" he asked.

"Come *here*," Jed instructed him in words like cut glass.

Gray watched as Jed pulled Velvet against his chest and brushed his cheek against her ear. The girl hadn't moved. Blowing out a tight breath of frustration, Gray moved in behind her, resting his hands on her waist, just above the Cajun's.

"Good," Jed murmured. "Now, raise your eyes and look over my shoulder. Two o'clock high."

Gray cut a glance up and to the right, squinting at the sky, trying to ignore Jed's lips moving intimately against Velvet's ear.

47

"Jeezis," Gray breathed.

There was something wrong with the sky. Irregular patches of shimmering white intruded into the powder blue heavens. Quickly, Gray scanned the horizon. They were everywhere. Grundian warships, camouflaged with reflected sunlight. How the fuck had they gotten past the Base sensor sweeps?

Jed nodded. "Velvet saw them," he whispered.

"You think they're close enough to hear us?"

Jed inclined his chin slightly. "And see us."

"What are they waiting for?" Velvet murmured.

Gray's heart expanded with fierce pride. There wasn't so much as a shimmer of fear in her voice. He tightened his hands on her waist. "They're still assembling," he answered.

"We need to get to Command," Jed stated.

Gray gave his head an imperceptible shake. "No time."

Jed's green eyes narrowed on his. "What then?"

Gray's mind raced. "Jason. Jason has the alarm codes. He lifted them for...last night."

Jed's eyes lightened a shade in understanding while Gray swiftly weighed options.

"Here's what we're going to do," he announced after scant seconds. "Jed, I'm going to throw a punch at you."

"How about we do that the other way around?" Jed muttered without moving his lips.

Gray snorted. "After I hit you, back off and stumble toward the hall. Tell Jason to activate the invasion alarm. Velvet, as soon as I hit the Cajun, you turn and run in the opposite direction. Get to Command. By the time you get there, the shields will be up. Tell them what's going on. They'll get the word out to the other bases."

"What about you?" Velvet asked, angling her head slightly to view him from the corner of her eye.

"Me?" Gray gave her a hard smile. "I'm gonna get a gunship. Meet me on the launch field and I'll take you for a ride."

* * * * *

The shields were up as Gray got his Hex lined up alongside those of his three wing companions, ready for liftoff. Following his barked orders, the field crew wheeled out the next wing of four Hexapods, hurrying to get them jockeyed into position and ready for launch. Gunship pilots were jogging onto the field as Gray threw open the entry hatches on each of the four ships. Match and Jason pelted toward him and disappeared inside their machines. Seconds later, Jed and Velvet raced across the field.

"Come on," Gray shouted at Velvet as he turned. Climbing into his ship, he left the hatch open for her then strapped himself into one of the two command seats. Both chairs were equipped with identical controls allowing the secondary pilot to take over should the first be injured. He reached overhead, flipping the necessary switches to initiate takeoff. "Go clear," he ordered. Sunlight crept into the ship as the Hex walls gradually became transparent. As Gray glanced down the line, Match was catapulted into the air. Then Jason. "Come on," Gray muttered, casting an impatient glance at the hatch door.

Where was she?

"Fuck," he cursed in the next instant as the Cajun's Hex whipped into the sky. "Fuck!" he shouted and smacked his fist down on the square launch button set into the left arm of his command seat.

The hatch door smacked closed and Gray hurtled into the air, spinning and tumbling as he streaked through the base shields. Designed to repel entry from without, the shields allowed the exit of ships, missiles or particle beams. Gray fingered the controls on the end of the chair's arms, whipping the Hex into a turn.

He laughed when he got his first good look at the crowded battlespace. Just beyond Earth's atmosphere, the dark sky was packed with Grundian spacecraft. No longer wasting energy on power-consuming camouflage, the enemy fleet was arrayed across the sky in all of its dark beauty. But that wasn't what made Gray laugh. He was laughing because the base shields must have gone up at the same moment the Grundians loosed their first barrage. Too close to the shields, the Grundian warships were caught in the reflected fire of their own weapons. Several of the lead ships were now reversing out of the fight, scarred from their own particle bursts and limping away like beaten dogs, their tails between their legs.

With a malicious smile on his lips, Gray went to work, attacking the weapon chutes on the battle cruisers, cutting and melting with the strafing fire of his twin particle beams.

A Hex shot past him, tumbling as the small gunship took some fire and spun it off. Gray only just dodged the reflected energy beam, his thumb sliding around the rolling ball set into the smooth plastech beneath his hand. After he'd sliced a gun barrel clean off an enemy battle cruiser, he looked around for a trace of pink in the crowded battlespace.

Jed's machine was pink. Unapologetically pink. Hot pink. The Cajun had imbued a bright tint of color into his ship's skin, distinguishing it from his companions' fighters when he was in go clear mode. When anyone was bold enough to give him a hard time about his choice of color, Jed would just shrug. "Down in Louisiana," he would drawl, "we splash the hot sauce on everything."

Cocky bastard. Jed acted like he'd *planned* the whole thing. It was a cover-up. Gray knew for a fact Jed hadn't known what color he'd end up with when he'd infused a trace of magnesium into the ship's skin.

Now Gray thought he caught a glimpse of the Cajun's Hex spinning away to his right. It disappeared behind the dark bulk of a huge destroyer. "Fuck," Gray growled, spinning to avoid small fire from a Grundian turret.

Where was she?

He stretched out his pinky, fingering the communications button set at the far edge of the command seat controls. He wasn't supposed to break communication silence during battle. History had long since proven that communication during high-speed Hexapod fighting was more distracting than helpful.

"Damn." Gray stabbed his finger at the button. "Cajun," he barked. "Do you have Velvet? Hammer out."

There was a short, stubborn silence. But Gray knew Jed couldn't resist the challenge. He wouldn't turn down an opportunity to match Gray's moxie. And he damn sure wouldn't let Gray break a rule without him.

"She's here," Jed fired back in two words.

Gray growled. "If you fuck with her, you're dead."

Jed responded with an amused snort. "Acknowledged," he drawled, "Cajun out."

Coming out of a spin, Gray flicked his gaze around him, scanning the skies for his next target.

His jaw dropped. He craned his neck as he searched the midnight skies.

The battlespace was empty.

The dark sky, previously littered with a thousand Grundian warships ranging in size from majestic battle cruisers to small pistol runners, was empty. Here and there on the blank backdrop were sprinkled pale blobs of light—his gunship companions, bobbing in empty space like fishing boats drifting across an endlessly open sea.

About thirty minutes later, Gray set his ship down next to Jed's machine. Through the transparent walls of his Hex, he watched a small group of airmen race to meet him. "Welcoming committee," he grunted to himself in the silence of the gunship. "Lieutenant Hamm saves the day." With a self-indulgent smile curling his lips, he stepped out of the

Hexapod. At that point, Gray's cocky grin died on his face. The welcoming committee was carrying stun guns.

A pretty Class One took a single step forward. "Lieutenant Hamm," she informed him, "you're under arrest. We're to accompany you to Command." Her stunner was pointed at his chest.

A low, rumbling growl built in his chest as his eyes narrowed on the nose of the gun, scant inches from his sternum. "Class One, you have exactly three seconds to get this thing *out* of my face. After that, it goes *up* your ass."

The young woman held her ground, though her eyes flickered with uncertainty.

Gray tempered his growl with a provocative smile. "Lower your weapon, sweetheart…and I'll let you accompany me anywhere you like."

Chapter Four

ဢ

Heavy boots scuffed on smooth concrete as Gray's escort ushered him off the launch field and through a low hangar. Men and women airmen stopped to stare as Gray's guard of four marched him across the yard toward headquarters. Gray set his mouth in a grim line and stared straight ahead. Inwardly, he fumed. Fucking typical! Save everyone's ass and you end up under arrest!

When they reached Command Headquarters, Gray's heart dropped as the group turned right and proceeded down the long, wide hall that led to the interrogation modules.

Being under arrest wasn't good but going to Interrogation was bad. Really bad.

The Class One motioned him through a large metal door. The harshly lit room was bare. As the heavy door closed silently behind him, Gray threw a scalding glance at the paneled wall in front of him. Although it didn't differ from the other three walls in appearance, Gray knew it was a two-way, made of the same material as his gunship. The blank, faceless wall hid a long observation room from which several interrogation modules could be observed. They could see him. He couldn't see them.

Like a caged tiger, Gray paced the room. The hot white light burned down on him from the ceiling panels overhead. His accusatory gaze strafed the two-way every time he turned. Where were the rest of his wing? Where were Jason and Match? Were they under arrest too? Cajun and Velvet? If he'd done anything to compromise his friends' careers he'd never forgive himself. Fuck. They'd never *let* him forgive himself.

Gray blew out a grim sigh. He was on a roll. First he'd compromised Velvet in her room. Now he was taking his entire team down with him. When things started going bad, they went all-the-way bad.

He turned sharply as one of the tall panels on the two-way wall cracked open. Sergeant Watson stood in the opening, beckoning him silently. What the fuck? He followed her into the observation room.

On the other side of the wall, the light was muted, cool and dim. It took a few seconds for Gray's eyes to adjust. When he could see clearly, he blinked several times. Command was seated at the long table centered in the large observation room! *I mean Command*! Everybody who was anybody was smiling as they stood to greet him. Commander Owens strode forward and grasped his hand warmly as an officer who outranked Gray by two degrees waited to put a cup of coffee in his hand.

"Thanks for saving our asses," the commander told him.

Perplexed, Gray shook the commander's hand as officers crowded around him. Jason grabbed Gray's hand next, a huge grin lighting his hazel eyes. Before Gray could finish shaking his hand, Matchstick yanked him away with an arm around his shoulders. Gray located Velvet standing behind Jed's chair. The Cajun was the only person in the room still seated. He acknowledged Gray with a casual, two-fingered salute that didn't rise above his coffee cup.

Lazy-assed bastard.

Gray turned back to his commanding officer. "Sir. Thank you. How did the rest of the planet fare?"

"We got the word out to the other bases but apparently this was the only base targeted. More about that later." Commander Owens motioned Gray to take a seat. "Are you hungry? Help yourself to sandwiches."

Gray hesitated long enough for Velvet to seat herself beside Jed. Sneaking a quick glance at her, he found her gaze fixed on the commander, her hands folded on the table in front of her. Quietly receptive, she appeared to be entirely at ease. At times, he could almost swear there were two Velvet Meadows — the cool version who could cut your heart out with a look and the warm, sultry version who had bucked beneath him as he'd hammered her into the door.

Hoping to catch a glimpse of the warm one he'd pounded into the door only hours earlier, Gray rounded the end of the table in a few long strides. As he moved behind the commander, he slipped her a look from beneath his dark eyelashes, snagging her gaze, letting his emotions, the heat of his passion and the depth of his longing burn in his eyes, hoping to spark something within her as he made eye contact.

Her only response was to shift closer to Jed.

Damn. Not exactly the reaction he was going for. Gray's fists clenched at his sides as he continued around the table.

Gray took the chair on Velvet's left and reached for the closest stack of sandwiches. He filled his mouth with soft fresh bread, tender ham and crisp Nefarian sprouts. He'd missed breakfast, wallowing in a morass of self-condemnation. Now that he knew he and his team weren't going to be turfed out of the Force, some of his appetite had returned. He chewed and swallowed and swigged down black coffee as officers arranged themselves in the seats around the table.

Surreptitiously, he cast a glance into Velvet's lap where her leg was nudged up against Jed's. His jaw tightened at the sight of Jed's wide muscular thigh cozied up against Velvet's slender one. Shifting his chair to the right a few inches, Gray opened his legs until his thigh pressed warmly against hers. When she fingered the hilt of her dagger, he called her bluff, opening his legs wider and crowding her some more.

"Sir," Gray asked. "Are we under arrest?"

"Yes, you are — at least as far as everyone else on the base is concerned."

"For lifting the invasion alarm codes?"

The commander shook his head. "For breaking communication silence."

Gray frowned as he questioned the commander with his gaze. You didn't get arrested for breaking communication silence.

"Your arrest is a cover, Lieutenant. We have a mission for you. Major Abel will fill you in."

A tall, smooth-skulled Cray leaned forward. His heavily muscled right arm rested on the table. The thick, stubby fingers of his right hand tapped on the table while the long, slender digits of his left curled around the handle of his coffee cup. "You, along with Lieutenant Meadows and Lieutenant Castille, are under arrest for breaking communication silence during battle. Tonight the three of you will escape. After fighting your way to your gunships, you'll make a run for space sector Delta."

The officer paused. "Don't kill anyone," he added as an aside.

Jed cleared his throat. "Why would we run on charges of a simple communication infraction?"

"Because, Lieutenant Castille, there was nothing *simple* about your communication infraction." The major gave the young officer a pointed look. "All of that will be explained if you'll just let me continue."

Jed lifted his hand, a typically arrogant gesture of assent.

"You'll be pursued, of course. We'll send forty Hexapods after you in a radial spray." The Cray waved a hand at Jason and Match. "Lieutenants Orlov and Maloney will launch out on your trajectory—they'll be right behind you. After forty-eight hours, we'll pull back all pursuit with the exception of your two friends. They'll claim to have a lead or a hunch as to your whereabouts and will be permitted to continue the chase."

Gray leaned forward in his chair, elbows on the table, hands clasped loosely before his face. "What's the mission's objective?" he asked.

"You'll make contact with the Grundians," Abel answered. "We hope to learn the whereabouts of their High Command."

Gray blew out a short snort of skepticism. "Begging your pardon, Sir. But isn't this all a little 'done before'? Fleeing the Alliance? Looking for the Grundians and passing ourselves off as renegade officers? Pretending to align ourselves with the enemy?" Gray shook his head. "The Grundians will never buy it."

Major Abel positively beamed. A warm wash of gold light glinted off the surface of his bald pate. "Normally, I'd agree with you, Lieutenant, except for one ironic turn of events. And you won't have to look for the Grundians, by the way. They'll find you. I'll let Officer Leeyu give you a little background."

A short Asian woman stood, her expression bright and animated. "This morning's attack wasn't a random skirmish," she informed Gray. Her short curtain of black hair swept her jawline as she bobbed her head. "The Grundians suspect we're developing a new weapon here on Earth Base Ten. In fact, they're right. Although several months away from completion, it's the sort of weapon that would put the Grundian plan of aggression out of business once and for all. It's a nonviolent explosion that would incapacitate all those of the Grundian race within its sphere of influence for twenty hours, allowing us to round them up, confiscate their ships and weapons and return them to their home planets. The Grundians don't know much about the weapon except what they've learned through their intelligence network. They assume it's a huge threat, deadly and catastrophic."

Officer Leeyu stopped to share a significant smile with her commanding officer. "Oh," she continued with an amused snicker, "and, after what happened during this morning's attack, we have to assume they also know the code name for the weapon."

Major Abel took up the discourse again. "Which brings us to the reason why the Grundians will come looking for you. It also explains why the Grundians disappeared from our airspace shortly after you broke communication silence. You see, Lieutenant Hamm, the code name for the new weapon is Velvet Hammer." Abel pushed a button on his workpad. "Let me play back the communication file we collected from your ship during this morning's encounter."

Gray caught the Cajun's gaze, sharing with him a brief second of revelation just before the major pushed a button and the audio file crackled to life.

"Cajun. Do you have Velvet? Hammer out."

"She's here."

"If you fuck with her, you're dead."

"Acknowledged. Cajun out."

Everyone in Command smiled as Abel chuckled. "When your communication was intercepted and translated, this is what the Grundians heard. *Cajun. Do you have Velvet Hammer out*, followed by your dire warning to Lieutenant Castille. Evidently the Grundians' translationware didn't pick up on the inflection in your voice. And what the Grundians heard scared the shit out of them. They thought Lieutenant Castille was carrying the new weapon."

Velvet frowned, shaking her head minutely. "Wouldn't they have found it strange that Lieutenant Hamm used feminine pronouns, referring to the weapon as *her* instead of *it*?"

Abel shrugged. "As Earthers, we have the unusual habit of using feminine pronouns for inanimate objects—for our ships, among other things. It's something the Grundians, and other species for that matter, can't understand. At any rate, they were evidently convinced Gray was talking about the weapon—convinced enough to hightail it out of our airspace."

Gray reached for a second sandwich and took a bite out of it, making sure that most of the bread's crisp crust fell into his lap.

The commander spoke up, guiding the conversation back to the subject at hand. "And that's why the Grundians will be so anxious to talk to you after your 'escape'. They'll think you're running from the Alliance due to your arrest. Normally, breaking communication silence wouldn't warrant an arrest but in this case they'll assume you were incarcerated for revealing the existence of the new weapon. They'll assume you know something about the Velvet Hammer. They might even hope to find a prototype on Lieutenant Castille's ship."

Gray nodded, holding the commander's gaze as he swept the crumbs from his lap, then continued on, cleaning the nonexistent crumbs from Velvet's thighs as well. A smile tugged at the corner of his lips when he heard her breath hiss out between her clenched teeth. "So after the Grundians find us, you think they'll take us to their High Command?"

Abel nodded. "For something this important, High Command will *insist* on seeing you. They won't let anyone less than the Main Inquisitor himself question you. This is a big opportunity for us. We've been trying to pinpoint their command post ever since they took out our base at Etiens but every time we think we're getting close, we lose them again."

"What do we know for certain about the location of the command post?" Gray asked, smoothing his palm over Velvet's knee and giving her thigh a squeeze.

Commander Owens leaned back in his seat. "Only that it's somewhere between the Delta and Epsilon quadrants."

"Epsilon!" His fingers tightened on Velvet's thigh—then flew to his mouth after a sharp blade pricked at the back of his hand. The lieutenant hadn't been bluffing after all. Gray sucked at the tiny sting of blood that colored the ridge of his knuckles.

The commander's mouth formed a hard line before he finally spoke. "The Grundians may be using the planet eYona as a base."

Two seats away from Gray, Jed stirred uncomfortably.

"I doubt the eYonan queen would permit that," Gray suggested as he lowered his fist to his thigh and rubbed his knuckles into his soft gray pants.

The commander shrugged. "eYona isn't part of the Alliance," he reminded Gray.

Stubbornly, Gray shook his head.

"They might be doing it without the queen's blessing," the commander countered, "possibly even without her knowledge." Commander Owens shifted in his seat. "But we may have misinterpreted the signals. The High Command *could* be headquartered on a roving space station or possibly even a battle cruiser, for that matter."

As the plan unfolded it was revealed that Gray would have tracer ions injected into his bloodstream—two elements combined to make a molecule that didn't occur naturally anywhere in the universe. The presence of those ions would allow Jason and Match to track him with a remote sensor sweep while following at a safe distance.

After making contact with the Grundians, Gray's party would almost certainly be transferred to the Grundian High Command. Jason and Match would follow, encrypt the coordinates and transmit them back to Earth. An alpha-class battle cruiser would set out from a nearby rendezvous point at a scale of one:thirty. Approximately forty-eight hours later, the Grundian High Command would be destroyed.

"Which gives you about two days to get out of there," Abel concluded.

Gray grunted. "And how are we supposed to pull that off?"

Major Abel smiled condescendingly. "Lieutenant Hamm, I wouldn't *for one moment* presume to tell you how to do your job. You and your team have proven yourselves resourceful in the past. We have every confidence in you. Your two wing companions, Orlov and Maloney, will be standing by to assist your escape."

Gray gave the officer a disgusted squint before shaking his head. "Thanks," he muttered. Leaning forward, he made eye contact with Sergeant Watson. "There's a chance they'll try to torture us for information. We'll need some meds."

The sergeant nodded. "We can get you some twelve-hour pain diminishers. You can take them just before you make contact with the Grundians. I trust all of your vaccinations are up to date?" Her quick glance took in Jed and Velvet, both of whom nodded.

"We've all been inoculated against truth serums," Gray agreed thoughtfully. "But they might threaten to kill one of us as inducement for the others to talk."

Officer Leeyu cut in swiftly. "Talk. You can tell them everything you know so far, along with a few other misleading tidbits we'll feed you. Of course, you don't want to appear too obliging. They'll get suspicious if you don't put up some sort of a fight."

Gray nodded. That was all well and good but if anyone so much as suggested they might hurt the girl, he was going to spill his guts. Truth, tidbits, the works. Gray knew his limit. And his limit was sitting beside him, her quiet amethyst gaze fixed on the commander.

The commander gave them about five seconds to absorb everything before he asked, "Any further questions?"

Gray nodded, drawing his mouth into a grim line as he braced himself. "I'd like to suggest a slight change in personnel. I see no reason for Lieutenant Meadows to accompany us on this mission."

Silence followed. Gray shot a remorseful glance at Velvet who turned her head and just about fried him with an amethyst beam of pure venom.

The commander's tone was flat. "Lieutenant Meadows was in Castille's Hexapod at the time of the communication infraction."

"*She* didn't break silence," Gray argued, his gaze hugging the table's surface. "*We* did."

The commander sighed. "Meadows is one of the Alliance's few Adepts, Lieutenant Hamm. As such, she could be an incredible asset to the mission. Do you have reason to believe she's unsuitable for the assignment? Physically or emotionally? Are you questioning the lieutenant's ability to perform?"

Gray opened his mouth. He wanted to lie. He wanted to tell them Velvet was emotionally unsuited. They'd probably buy it. He could tell them about her tendency toward cold violence. How she'd attacked him—a fellow officer—just that morning in the mess hall. Gray fingered the fresh mark on his neck while Velvet glared a warning at him.

He could tell them about the scars she carried with her. Etiens. About her notebook and what it meant to her. How dependent she was on the memories it enshrined. Gray swallowed a hard lump of emotion. How hungry she was for a tender word, a gentle touch. How he'd broken her with one kiss. How he'd shattered her with one deception. Worded the right way, Gray could probably get her a nice long stint in repo—where she'd be perfectly safe. Perfectly safe and alive and despising him for the rest of his miserable existence.

Ah, shit.

Gray shook his head, his voice hoarse as he lowered his gaze to the tabletop again. "No, Sir. That's not the problem. I don't doubt the lieutenant's ability to perform. It's my own performance that should be under scrutiny. I don't think I can work with the lieutenant. If she's threatened, I'll talk, Sir."

The commander's eyebrows winged upward. "You've worked with women in the past, Lieutenant. I don't see how this situation is going to be any different."

Gray nodded, his eyes downcast. "This is going to be different, Sir." He raised his gaze to his commander's face. "Because I'm in love with Lieutenant Meadows."

Chapter Five

Gray pressed his lips together into a hard line. That ought to do it. A public declaration of love, rattled off in the company of his entire Command. If that didn't convince Velvet that he was sorry about what he'd done last night, then nothing would.

The commander looked embarrassed for Gray. Shit! Gray felt embarrassed for himself. He swallowed hard, his gaze on the commander but his attention fixed firmly on the woman beside him.

She didn't react in any way whatsoever.

He shouldn't have been surprised. This was the woman who'd seen her entire unit decimated at Etiens and walked away with a notebook under her arm. This was the woman who'd sliced away five inches from her hair when she would have been justified in cutting off his fingers. This was the woman who, betrayed and compromised, had shown up in the mess hall that morning looking sexy enough for a quick fuck—more offended than hurt—dry-eyed and virtually emitting sparks as she shrugged off the man who'd betrayed her in bed.

And this was the woman who Gray had followed outside into the yard, who'd picked out the camouflaged warships, despite her pique. And when he'd given her his instructions in a few words, he'd *known* she would carry them out without hesitation. *Known* that he could depend on her to perform coolly under fire and carry out her objective despite their personal differences.

Gray shifted his gaze sideways to the Cajun. A faint sneer of superiority curled his lip, a sneer that suggested Gray was the most pathetic thing Jed had ever set eyes on.

The commander cleared his throat as he moved his gaze to Officer Leeyu.

The short woman looked thoughtful for a moment. "There's nothing they've heard here that they can't repeat," she informed the commander.

The commander turned his face and settled his gaze on Gray again. "Is there anything else?" he asked into the silence.

Gray shook his head grimly.

Commander Owens lifted one eyebrow and turned his gaze on Velvet. His eyes glittered with barely contained amusement. His fist covered his mouth for several seconds before he shifted it enough to ask, "Lieutenant Meadows, do you wish to excuse yourself from the mission?"

Velvet's sun-washed hair shifted as she shook her head and answered, "No, Sir. I'm certain Lieutenant Hamm's condition is temporary. I'll do everything I can to change his mind about me. I'm sure he'll recover from his infatuation as soon as he realizes the sentiment is *not* returned."

"Good," the commander clipped out. "The mission will go ahead as planned. Lieutenant Hamm, as wing leader you're in command of the operation."

Gray slumped in his chair. His response to his superior was automatic and correct. "Thank you, Sir."

✳ ✳ ✳ ✳ ✳

"Just head for space sector Delta," Gray grumbled in a lisping Cray accent, "the Grundians will find *you*. Yeah, right." With his teeth, he ripped a chuck off his chicken cordon bleu bar and let it heat up on his tongue.

They were fourteen hours into their escape, their gunships locked together as they skimmed through space in perspective drive, scale of one:twenty.

Frustrated with the situation in general, Gray rubbed his knuckles over his unshaven jaw as he slipped his gaze to his right. Velvet was floating upside down, her nose hovering about eight inches from Jed's face.

She'd braided the uneven strands of her silken hair into a single bristling plait and it arched under her head like a pale serpent. With her amethyst gaze fixed on the Cajun, Velvet was doing a very convincing job of ignoring Gray.

Command had supplied her with a new tie before they'd made their escape fourteen hours earlier. Gray snorted. Command wouldn't want a renegade officer fleeing the Force in anything less than full military attire. But when *he'd* requested a clean shirt to replace the one with the bloodstained collar, Jed had spoken up before Command could answer, suggesting that the blood would help support their story that they'd fought their way out of Earth Base Ten.

Damn Jed, anyhow. He'd only done it to irk Gray.

Jed tugged on the end of her braid and she floated closer. "Hey, beautiful," he murmured.

Swallowing the bite in his mouth, Gray tamped down the nasty growl that rumbled in his chest. "Feel free to move to the other pod," he suggested brusquely. With a flick of his fist, he pointed his energy bar at the open hatchway leading to Jed's empty machine.

"Feel free to stay right here," Jed countered with a snort. "Don't let the Hammer chase you off."

"I wasn't talking to *her*," Gray growled.

"Hey," Jed drawled with a laugh, "no need to chase me off, either. Anything you wanna say to Velvet you can say to me."

"No, I can't," Gray shot at him.

"Why not?"

"Because I don't *want* to fuck you."

Jed's lips thinned into a conciliatory smile. He unwrapped his own energy bar and took a bite of peppercorn steak.

Ignoring his wing companion, Gray swiveled in his chair. "Listen, Velvet. There are two things you should know. First off, when we were together in your room, I moved you out of the camera's visual range."

The expressive line of her eyebrow lifted into an arch. "So that's why you fucked me up against the door. And here I thought you were just being romantic."

Gray ground his teeth then continued. "In addition, nobody ever *saw* anything because they turned the workpad off before we even got started. Right, Cajun?"

Jed leaned back in his command seat, his legs spread in a casual male stance. "I have no idea. I wasn't there."

Gray steamed. "Oh, yeah. I forgot you were so *fucking* noble."

Jed blew out a short, cynical snort. "I wasn't being noble, you fucking prick. I was just being *decent*."

"Boys, boys," Velvet murmured. She gave Jed a warm smile that just about had Gray going thermo-nova. "Thanks for being decent," she told Jed.

Jed's gaze softened as he looked at her. With one finger beneath her chin, he tilted it downward. "I'm not that decent," he confessed contradictorily. "I'd have watched him with another woman. I was just pissed it wasn't me in your room."

Velvet's smile sweetened. "Well then, thank you for being so honest."

Disgusted, Gray stared at the two of them, cooing like fucking lovebirds. Jeezis. The Cajun could do no wrong! If Jed called her a slut, she'd probably send him a thank you note. It was sickening. Gray was tired of their flirting. Finishing off his energy bar, he punched a series of commands into the controls over his head.

"What are you doing?" Jed challenged him.

"Setting a course for Delta Base Twenty," Gray answered.

Jed's eyes narrowed in thought. "What are you planning?"

"There's a Tauran teahouse on the base."

Velvet's brow wrinkled up into a questioning frown while Jed snorted out a soft bark of laughter. "Don't stop now," he drawled. "I wanna hear the rest of this."

"I'm tired of waiting for the Grundians to find us. I say we give them a hand."

Jed's gaze slipped to Velvet. "Are you sure you want to do that? Command said—"

"Screw Command. I'm making a command decision. Jason and Match are tracking us."

"But the Taurans are neutral," Velvet interjected.

"That's what they'd like you to believe," Gray grunted. "They might not be allied with the Grundians but that hasn't stopped them from supplying our enemy with everything from popcorn to polyrounds."

Jed sneered as he waved his peppercorn steak in the air for emphasis. "So you're gonna take Velvet into a teahouse full of Tauran males. You *do* know that Taurans have tusks on their dicks?"

"They won't touch her if I mark her first."

"Mark me?" Velvet spoke up, her eyes narrowing with suspicion. "What do you mean, mark me?"

The cabin was silent as Gray hit the enter button.

She targeted the Cajun with her gaze. "What does he mean, mark me?" she demanded.

The Cajun just shook his head, a dissatisfied expression twisting his hard lips.

Releasing the seat's restraints, Gray launched himself away from the chair and through the air toward the hatchway opening. On the way, he reached out and snagged the end of Velvet's long braid. She cursed with surprise as she wriggled in the air. With one hand on the hatch opening, Gray towed her toward Jed's pod.

"I'm going to sleep," he informed her, "and you're sleeping with me."

She stopped squirming and turned her head around to glare at him. "You're nuts if you think I'm going to sleep with you, you jumped-up space Neanderthal."

Gray shook his head. "I'm in command of this operation and, as your CO, I'm ordering you to sleep at the same time I do. I'm not leaving you alone with the Cajun," he added with a growl. "He has a bad reputation."

Jed whistled out a long trilling note. "Good idea," he sang with cynicism. "Save her for the Taurans."

"*He* has a bad reputation!" Velvet exclaimed. "What the hell do you have?"

Gray smirked as he trawled her along behind him. "You've already seen what I have. He has the reputation. I have the hammer."

The sleeping compartment was a small cylindrical space in the middle of the ship, the walls quilted with air cushioning. Once inside the sleeping chamber, Gray glanced over his shoulder to scowl at Jed through several layers of transparent walls. "Go opaque," he ordered with a growl.

Velvet glowered at him across the small space that separated them.

"We need to talk," he stated.

"About?"

"About what happened between us back in your room at Earth Base Ten. We...shared something special back there."

Her face was like a mask. A beautiful, emotionless mask. "I'll allow that it could have been special, Lieutenant Hamm. But whatever we had is gone. Completely. Irrevocably. Gone."

Gray ground his teeth, resisting the urge to snarl. "Listen. When I...planned that whole thing, I didn't know you weren't..."

"Didn't know what?" she cut at him, her eyes brilliant with purple fire. "You didn't know I wasn't a slut? You didn't know I wasn't a bitch? If I were, do you think it would have justified your actions? Because I'm having a hard time thinking of any woman who would have deserved what you tried to do to me."

Gray nodded, gritting his teeth, struggling for words. "I didn't know you were so..."

"Don't!" she stopped him with an outstretched palm. "Don't you *dare* pity me for my weakness, for what *you* saw as my vulnerability. Quit now while you're ahead, Lieutenant. You can't shovel your way out of this shit. You're just digging your own grave."

"Velvet, I didn't mean to hurt you. I didn't think you were a slut. I didn't think you were a bitch. I just thought—"

"Do you know what I think?" Velvet sliced back with ice in her voice. "I think you've spent so much of your life lying, you've convinced yourself that you're good at it." Her cold gaze dropped to sub-zero. "Now pay attention, Lieutenant Hamm. Whatever I felt for you back on Earth Base Ten is gone, dead, long cold and buried. You buried it. Deal with it."

As Gray watched, she twisted her head and the rest of her body slowly rotated to the padded wall behind her. "How do I keep from drifting into you while we sleep?" she demanded, as though the prospect was the most distasteful thing she could possibly imagine.

"You haven't spent much time in space," Gray stated gruffly.

She shook her head as her body slowly turned toward him again. "I was on the ground crew at Etiens. I'm a weapons trainer."

"Let me guess. Knives?"

"Among other things."

Gray nodded at the padded walls. "Well, Miss Knives-Among-Other-Things, if you don't want to free-float, you can use the restraints."

Velvet scanned the walls around her. "What restraints?"

Gray pushed away from the wall behind him and floated toward her, catching her body between his outstretched arms and bearing her back against the cushioned wall. He let his lips brush the side of her cheek, his stubble graze across her jawline as he pressed her into the wall.

Her breath was a welcome wash of warmth at the base of his throat as he tucked his chin into his neck and smiled down at her. "These restraints," he murmured.

Gray reached around behind her and demonstrated the clear plastech bands that stretched across every diamond-shaped pillow tucked against the gently curving wall. He pulled the soft, pliable plastech out several inches while using the leverage to push her farther into the wall. "There are enough here that you can restrain yourself in almost any position," he suggested in a sexy rumble, shifting his hips and grinding his thick erection into her mound. "Spread eagle on your back with your legs wide open or tucked over on your side, leaving your adorable little ass accessible for a rear —"

"Get off me, you ass!" Gathering her legs into her chest, Velvet kicked him across the chamber.

He rubbed a hand over his upper abdomen and gave her an unapologetic grin. "Most people just anchor themselves with one arm so they still have some freedom of movement," he laughed.

She reached for one of the bands and pulled herself to the wall. With a doubtful expression, she slipped her arm through the restraint, all the way to her biceps. She looked at Gray who was still floating. "Do me a favor and restrain yourself," she told him.

"Sweetheart," he muttered, "I already am."

Her retort was sharp. "What do you mean by that, exactly?"

Gray snorted as he slipped his arm through one of the bands on the wall directly opposite her. He'd forgotten about her *super hearing.* "Believe me, princess. I'm already using a whole lot of restraint."

"I'm guessing you'd like to kick my ass?" she suggested tightly.

"You got that *half* right," he muttered.

"What was that?"

"I'm sorry," he prevaricated insincerely, "did you say kick or fuck?"

"Kick," she answered with a snort.

"In that case, I'll pass for now. Let me know if you want to change your offer."

"It *wasn't* an offer," she growled.

Gray smiled as she crossed a leg over her body and hooked her ankle into one of the restraints. She was a stubborn little handful, full of cold fire. When she closed her eyes, he gazed at her elegant profile—the sharp line of her proud chin, the delicious pout of her lips, her fine, straight nose, the delicate ridge of her brow, her thick lashes resting on her cheek. She was a beauty, all right.

And she had his heart by the short and curlies.

Too bad she hated him.

Of course, that might work in his favor. He might still be able to make her drop out of the mission. As much as she disliked him, she might refuse to be marked, giving him an excuse to kick her off the team and leave her on Delta Base Twenty…where she'd be relatively safe.

The fact was, the idea of Velvet in the hands of the Grundians turned his spine to water. If anything happened to her, he'd never be able to live with himself. If anything happened to her *and he had to watch,* he'd go stark, barking mad.

Gray sighed as he gazed across the dimly lit sleeping chamber. He was getting harder just looking at her. Reaching down, he readjusted his stubbornly interested shaft and closed his eyes.

* * * * *

Jed smiled lazily as he stared across the cabin at the open hatch door. He'd seen the look on Velvet's face as the Hammer had dragged her through the opening. Gray wasn't getting any. Served the bastard right. Jed finished his energy bar and closed the wrapper inside the trash chute.

With his hands clasped behind his neck and his knees spread, he considered Gray's parting words. Yeah, Jed had a reputation, though there was a reason for his cavalier attitude toward sex. He'd kept his relationships short and sweet, never encouraging the women who were interested in him. He never spent more than one night with a woman and never the *entire* night. A few hours of mutual satisfaction and he was gone. Jed had a good reason for keeping his distance, especially where female officers were concerned.

Spaceforce women were smart. It wouldn't take much for one of them to recognize him for what he was. And Jed had waited too long and worked too hard to blow his cover over a woman. It hadn't been easy, eradicating his accent and falsifying the documents that would get him a berth at Spaceforce. If Gray had ever stopped to wonder why Jed was so good at getting past mechanical door locks, lifting codes and cheating his way past firewalls, he might have started getting suspicious. Jed had perfected those arts long before he was ever admitted as a Spaceforce cadet, sometimes breaking into Command Headquarters for the sole purpose of planting his own false documents in files and on computers.

He brushed aside the inconvenient surge of guilt that crept up on him, challenging his sense of right and wrong.

Deep down, he didn't like the fact that he was betraying the one thing he valued and respected above all else. He might be doing the wrong thing but he was doing it for the right reasons. At least that's what he told himself. If he ever got caught he'd just have to cross that bridge when he came to it.

Reaching inside his jacket, he pulled a thin piece of filmboard from his interior pocket. He turned it over in his hands, leaning back in his chair before he held it up to the light, checking it for imperfections.

After he'd broken into Velvet's room, he'd stopped by Gray and Jason's room. The door to their dorm had opened just as easily as Velvet's had. Only this time, he hadn't come away empty-handed—though it took him a while to find Gray's computer. At first, it had appeared as though the Hammer had taken his workpad to breakfast with him—however unlikely that might have been. A gleam of reflected light had drawn his eye to the wastebasket beneath Gray's workstation where Jed had found the broken remains of his computer.

The hard drive looked good to him. It was hard to kill the new flexible filmboards.

He palmed it into one of the ports on the console in front of him and pushed a button to access the drive. He found the file he wanted right away, though there were only a few minutes of useful data.

Velvet sitting on her bed, hugging her notebook.

Gray sitting beside her, flipping through the pages while Velvet watched them turn.

Jed nodded as he zoomed in her face. "There you are," he murmured.

He grimaced as Gray fell over her on the bed. Moments later, Jed was tilting his head as her small breast came into view—plump, pretty and round. His lips parted for an instant as he drew in a long, shallow breath. As Jed watched the monitor on the control console, Gray's fingers dragged over

Velvet's nipple and cupped her small tit, lifting its weight into his large, rough hand. When his thumb grazed across the pebbled surface, her nipple rose for him, jutting into his hand as he pulled his palm over her areola.

Responding to the sensually erotic visual, Jed curled his fingers, digging his fingertips into his palms as his cock stretched inside his pants. His view was obscured in the next frame when Gray dragged Velvet off the bed and out of the picture. Jed pushed out a rough sigh, leaning forward in his command seat. He could imagine what happened next. He didn't need to listen. He skipped forward and stopped.

The dorm super asking Gray to leave.

He skipped forward again.

Velvet sleeping. Velvet waking up. Velvet finding the filmcam. Her face.

"And there you go," he muttered with a slight growl.

He leaned back in his chair again, rubbing his cock. The erotic visual of Gray panting over Velvet had started a slow burn that weighed heavily in his crotch. Ignoring the inconvenient sting of arousal, he mused vaguely. What would it be like to watch almost a hundred of your comrades die while the polyrounds crashed around you in a deafening roar of heat and death? How would an Adept react to protect her mind from the terrifying assault, the slow, agonizing destruction of all she loved? Would her shields have gone up? Perhaps unconsciously? How long would it take before the shields came down again? Would her Adept heart ever allow her to love again?

Gray had fucked up big time. Alone with her in her room, he'd managed to pull Velvet out of the hard shell of protection that her unique Adept traits had built up around her. But when she'd found that camera stuck to her desk...

Poor kid. Under the circumstances, Jed wished that he'd stopped Gray from going to her room that night. Either that or warned her—as hard as that would have been. Rivalry amongst wing companions was one thing. Outright betrayal was another.

Chapter Six

ℌ

As the airmen sauntered into the main hub of Delta Base Twenty, Gray wrinkled his nose, drawing in a lungful of the space station's stale, over-circulated atmosphere. "Not exactly up to Earth Base standards," Gray muttered.

"Not by a long shot," Velvet agreed. "The gravity's a shade on the light side too."

"So, what's the plan?" Jed asked.

Gray rubbed a hand over his stubbled jaw. "I want a shower, either that or a quick slash—before we go to the teahouse and get ourselves captured."

The Hexapods were equipped with only the most rudimentary bathing facilities which did *not* include a shower or anything remotely *like* a shower. Gray hadn't bathed in thirty-odd hours, since the morning he'd returned from Velvet's room. The next step up from the Hexapod's cleansing bidet would be a slashroom. Gray grimaced at the idea of the tiny stall with its brief slash of cleansers. Although that might be all the space station hostelries would have to offer, he was hoping for a real shower with real water—warm water.

"Captured?" Jed queried with a growl.

"The Grundians will have offered a reward for our capture. All we need to do is find a Tauran who's heard about it."

Gray halted at a directory beacon and spoke the words, "Rooms for rent." The pylon flashed out four long beams of light indicating different directions. A line of characters rode along the colored beams, indicating the amenities offered at each of the four hostelries on Delta Base Twenty.

"Rooms rented by the hour. Earther spoken here," Gray read aloud. "Works for me," he grunted, steering Velvet into one of the corridors radiating from the central hub.

They rented a small room with one bed, taking turns in the full gravity shower. Gray went in after Jed, dallying under the spray of hot water, thinking about Velvet, soaping his cock absently, pulling his slippery hands over his length, playing it out to its full eleven point five inches. Its heavy weight dragged the fat head downward so that the thick rod swung almost perpendicular to his body.

Watching the dark vein that snaked down the centerline of his shaft, Gray stroked his cock a few times as he sighed. He could have kicked himself for screwing this up with Velvet. Her hot tight pussy was the sweetest thing he'd ever dipped his hammer into. And to think she would have been able to take all of him eventually! It was enough to make a grown man cry.

And if that wasn't enough to move him to tears, there was the painfully sweet memory of Velvet, her clean sparkling scent as she rolled beneath him, her sweet salty taste as he dragged his mouth over her satiny flesh. Her small murmuring cries as he drove into her. Her teeth in his earlobe, nipping sharply as she came. Her beautiful hot sheath tightening on his cock. Her eyes shocked wide as he rode her through orgasm. Then afterward. Her lips brushing along his jawline. Her thick lashes resting against her cheek just before she opened her eyes and looked up at him. Her amethyst gaze reaching deep into his heart and flinging wide a door that had never so much as been cracked open before that night.

He'd fallen in love in one instant and thrown it away in the next, injuring her so deeply that he could only pray for some sort of divine intervention. She was never going to forgive him. In the meantime he was stuck, dangling at the tail end of love, hanging on to a faint hope for forgiveness by a pretty slim thread. Gray slumped against the wet porcelain wall, squeezing his eyes shut, groaning at the dull ache that echoed in his heart and pulsed in the thick root of his cock.

He stepped out of the shower, staring down at his erection, tempted to put the poor beast out of its misery with a few pumps of his fist. With a shake of his head, he discarded the idea as he reached for a towel. He'd need his erection a bit later, when it was time to mark her.

After toweling himself dry, he pressed his dick up against his belly and wrapped the thin, absorbent fabric tightly around his waist. Velvet was on the other side of the bathroom door, waiting her turn to shower. He purposefully brushed against her, the heavy mist from the tiny bathroom enveloping them both in a provocative male warmth which he hoped she'd respond to.

She continued into the bathroom without so much as a flicker of emotion.

For at least five seconds he stared at that closed door, tempted to follow her into the musky, male-scented room, back her up against the steamy porcelain wall, plant his hands either side of her head and rub his rough jaw into the hollow at the base of her throat—*make* her acknowledge his presence, his sex appeal *and* his full arousal.

Not necessarily in that order.

"Fuck," he growled, glaring at the offensive door before he took a step sideways into the room. There, he found Jed's taunting smile targeting his own lust-wrenched expression.

"She's a beauty," Jed murmured quietly, his voice oddly devoid of cynicism. "Isn't she?"

Gray just stared at him for several seconds, waiting for a snide follow-up, expecting the Cajun to remind him how he'd fucked things up with Velvet. When Jed remained silent, Gray just nodded helplessly.

"What's wrong?" Jed asked.

"Nothing," Gray answered. "Everything. I just don't like the whole situation. If she's threatened…I'll kill myself trying to get to her."

"I won't stand in your way," Jed told him with a careless yawn.

"Thanks," Gray muttered. "It's nice to know you can count on your friends."

"You're welcome," Jed murmured back at him.

* * * * *

Gray had just tucked his pants into his heavy leather boots and was about to reach for his shirt when Velvet sashayed through the bathroom door—entirely naked. Her uniform, which she'd worn into the bathroom, hung over her slim forearm, hiding absolutely nothing.

Nothing that counted, at any rate.

His jaw dropped as he glared at the pale, sunny wisps on her mound. The little chit was displaying her wares, flaunting her naked body in front of Jed—apparently with no other purpose than to goad Gray. He pulled his hands back through his damp hair. "What are you doing?"

She lifted her slim shoulders with casual grace. "Nothing you haven't seen before," she pointed out. She smiled at the Cajun, stretched out on the single bed. "Nothing I don't want Jed to see."

Gray whipped the thin towel from around his neck and flung it at her. "Well, there's plenty there that *I* don't want Jed to see. Cover yourself up," he demanded.

She tossed her clothes on the bed at Jed's feet, smiling at the Cajun as she shook the towel out like a provocative little matador.

A thin sheen of red clouded Gray's vision as she turned her back to him, presenting to him the firm white apple of her derriere. His cock, already primed and ready for action,

80

throbbed in thickening pulses while he envisioned bending her over the bed, splitting her cheeks with the drive of his cock and shafting her right to the core.

If she wasn't careful, Gray was going to take a bite out of that fine white flesh.

When Jed returned her smile from behind half-closed eyes, Gray was just about ready to knock the Cajun's teeth down his throat. His fists bunched at his sides for a brief, angry second. He drew a deep breath, shook out his fingers and slashed a hand through the air. There was a sharp smack as his hand connected with Velvet's elegant little ass.

She turned on him swiftly, just about spitting fire, her fingers white where she clenched the towel at her side.

He gave her a slow smile. "Just checking to see if the pain diminishers have kicked in yet."

"I haven't taken my dose yet!"

"Well, don't forget," he drawled.

He saw her hand coming. He didn't try to stop it, though he could have if he'd wanted to. He figured it was best to let her go ahead and get her revenge in now. He didn't want her sticking a knife between his ribs later on.

He didn't flinch when her palm stung his cheek. He'd taken *his* pain diminishers.

"Thanks for the reminder," she bit out at him.

"Not a problem," he muttered. His hand shot out and trapped her delicate wrist. Slowly, he pulled her hand back to his face, rubbing her knuckles into the stubble on his cheek where she'd smacked him. When she tried to yank away from him, he tightened his grip, drawing her small hand to his mouth and pressing a kiss into her palm. "Not a problem at all," he growled.

Her eyes were pure crystalline fire as she glared up at him. Jeezis, she was a hot little package. Riled and naked. What a provocative combination. She might not know it but she was about one inch from getting nailed to the wall.

81

He released her wrist reluctantly and watched as she backed away from him toward the narrow bed tucked against the wall.

Jed's gaze smoothed over her ass as he drawled, "You might as well let her tease, Hammer. She has to be marked before we go to the tearoom anyhow."

Velvet turned and gave Jed a wary look as she dropped the towel and reached for her black thong. Gray's large handprint glowed across her bottom in a splash of deep pink. It looked good on her. If it weren't for Jed's presence, he'd have gone down on his knees then and there, gathered her legs into his chest and pressed a kiss of penitence onto her adorable little ass—right there where his hand had heated her skin into a warm blush.

"Marked?" she asked.

Gray answered her before Jed could open his mouth. "We're about to go into a tearoom full of Tauran males. You can't go in there unmarked. You're a blonde. They'll tear you apart trying to claim you."

His jaw tightened when she didn't even turn to acknowledge his explanation. Instead, Velvet kept watching the Cajun as she stepped into her thong and pulled it up her legs. A narrow black line split her cheeks as she leaned over and snagged her knee pants. Gray rubbed a hand into the spray of dark hair on his chest, growling as he watched Jed's eyes follow the light bounce of her breasts.

"The Hammer's right," Jed told her, rolling to sit on the edge of the bed. "Taurans can't resist a female with fair hair. One of us is gonna have to mark you."

"*One of us?*" Gray exploded with a rumbling snarl. "Don't get any ideas, Cajun. In this case, *one of us* means me!"

But Velvet continued to ignore Gray, her gaze fixed on the Cajun as she pulled her regulation pants up over the sweeping line of her hips. "What do you mean by marked?"

"The Taurans won't touch you if you're carrying the scent of another male."

Velvet just stared while Jed put her bra in her hand.

"If you smell like you just had sex," Jed explained bluntly. "If you're wearing another man's cum."

Velvet took a sharp step backward. Her bra dangled from the fingers hiding behind her derriere. Her defensive reaction pulled her shoulders back, pushing her breasts forward. Gray's mouth watered at the memory of her nipples stiffening inside his mouth, their soft pebbled texture, her sweet salty flavor as he licked her areolas and sucked her nipples. Those tits belonged to *him*.

"No way," she said.

"Fine," Gray barked, throwing his hands into the air. "You're out of the mission then. You can wait here for us." Which was all-fucking-right with him. She'd be much better off camping out at the space station than captured by the Grundians.

Jed's keen green gaze cut toward him. The Cajun's normally half-closed eyes cracked open a shade wider as if to emphasize his point. "The Grundians will be looking for two men and a *woman*," he argued.

"She *has* to be marked," Gray insisted right back.

The room filled with a tense silence as the two men glared at each other. Finally Velvet's voice intruded into the weighty stillness. "You're not cutting me out of this mission," she lashed out at Gray.

"You're not going anywhere unless you're marked," Gray told her.

Her eyes darted between the two men as she chewed on her bottom lip. "Jed," she said finally. "I'll let the Cajun mark me."

Jed's head snapped around to stare at Velvet. Without thinking, he checked her eyes. But there was nothing there. He looked at Gray next. Plenty there. Gray was going to *kill* him. Quickly, he collected himself as he drew a long, slow breath in through his nose.

Those six words from Velvet had just about floored him. Even though he was the one who'd suggested the idea, he hadn't expected to react so strongly to the sound of those provocative words on Velvet's lips — asking that he mark her, agreeing to wear his cum. The request made a hard pulse of yearning surge into his groin, thickening his shaft and weighing heavily in his balls.

Jed was just as Neanderthal as the next guy — the next guy being Gray — and he knew it. But he found the mental image of Velvet stripped naked and pressed against him vastly satisfying as he imagined himself stroking his cock to the edge of release then rubbing his shaft into her belly and emptying out on her skin — grinding his lower body against hers as the warm wash of cum spread over their sex-heated skin and sealed them together like a wet kiss.

The idea was pure dirty eroticism.

But the idea affected more than his dick, he discovered as he stood there suspended in heart-pounding, breath-holding wonder. He'd been waiting for this — or something like this — ever since he'd seen Velvet in the mess hall forty-six hours ago. *By the Princess*, he'd been waiting for this. Even knowing that Gray had already staked his claim on the lovely Adept. Even knowing that Gray had already *fucked* her. "Oh great," he complained, trying to find his voice, "make me whack off in front of the biggest dick in the Force. Are you *trying* to make me feel inadequate?"

His comment was meant to make her smile. Jed had a dick with a barrel like a blastuka. At least that's what his last bedmate had cooed at him just before she wrapped her lips around his cock and blew him out. But his attempt at humor was lost on Velvet. In her anxiety, she nervously disregarded his words.

Back to business.

Jed had to assume that Gray would probably prefer to leave Velvet behind at the space station. No doubt, he was concerned for her safety. Apparently—and probably for the first time in his life—Gray was letting his heart get in the way of his normally keen judgment. Normally, Gray was sharp, quick and decisive. You didn't become wing leader unless you could make the right decisions and make them fast.

It wasn't a bad thing that Gray was thinking with his heart. But the mission was important. More important than Gray's obvious weakness for Velvet. The chance to wipe out the Grundian High Command was the sort of mission every airman dreamed of, as well a hugely worthwhile goal. If the mission were successful, millions of lives might be saved. And, though he didn't realize it, Gray was underestimating Velvet as a woman *and* an officer. By the Princess, she was a Spaceforce lieutenant!

Then there was Velvet to consider. Gray didn't know it yet but the girl's emotional and mental well-being was at stake. Velvet was going to need some help if she was ever going to cast off her emotional shields and find her way back to real life.

"Maybe we should both mark you," Jed suggested casually while watching her closely. "Alpha Tango," he added quietly in answer to Gray's snarl.

She drew herself up with a steadying breath. Her eyes flicked toward the bathroom door. "Both of you, then. Leave it in the sink," she answered.

Jed breathed out a silent sigh of relief. "Gray?" he invited with a hand sweeping toward the bathroom door.

Gray was angry. He didn't even close the door behind him. From where Jed sat watching Velvet slip into her bra and shirt, he could hear the sound of slapping flesh as Gray pumped his cock. A few seconds of silence followed as Velvet shifted uneasily. Jed held her eyes, encouraging her with a relaxed smile. Moments later, Gray stalked from the tiny bathroom, his jaw set, a line of lust and anger shadowing his cheekbones.

In the bathroom, Jed found the sink painted with Gray's cum, long thick ropes of milky ejaculate. He closed the door, waiting a few minutes before opening it again. He called for Velvet while he dabbled his fingers in Gray's cum. She appeared at the door with Gray glaring behind her, dissatisfaction darkening his eyes. The storm brewing in his heated gaze muted somewhat when he saw the sink and realized what Jed had done—or what he hadn't done, to be precise. From his place in the doorway, the Hammer narrowed his eyes and shot Jed a look that said *what the fuck?*

Jed gave him a grim smile in return. With Gray's semen on his fingertips, Jed brushed Velvet's hair away from her neck and dabbed the cum behind first one ear then the other. "You're gonna like this," he told her with a soft rumble. "Eau de Cajun Hammer."

Her nostrils flared and her lips thinned as she held her breath.

"That should do it," he murmured, stepping away from her.

As though he'd been supporting her, she stumbled forward. Both men reached for her at the same time, steadying her as she wrapped her slender fingers around Jed's wrist. Her gaze was apologetic as their eyes connected. For the tiniest space of time, something flickered in the depths of her dark irises. Momentarily stunned, Jed's eyes widened as his heart rate quickened. He quelled the groan that was on his lips, forcing a smile back on his mouth as he whispered, "Hold on, sweetheart. I've got you."

Talk about bad timing! The flicker of interest that Jed had hungered to see warming her gaze—for him—was finally there. For one fraction of a heartbeat it had glowed deep in her shadowed irises, smoldering beneath a provocatively female vulnerability that had his heart doing back flips.

It was there and he couldn't act on it.

She belonged to Gray. The same Gray who was standing behind her at that very moment.

He leaned forward as much as he dared, capturing her warmth on his chest, soaking up the feel of her, reveling in that stolen moment of contact. Her soft breasts pillowed against his upper abs as he pressed her against Gray. He liked the sensation — the closeness. And perhaps not surprisingly, it lost nothing for Gray being there at her back. He liked the whole package, the whole situation — Gray, Velvet and himself — the slender female trapped between the two men.

It wasn't hard to imagine both men fucking the dainty female held captive between them — Gray buried in her ass while Jed fed his cock into the warm, wet slit between her silken thighs. Gray's breath blasting from his lungs and dampening Jed's hair. Jed's thighs, hard with muscle, dusted with sweat, straining and stiff as they rubbed into Gray's thick legs. Jed holding Velvet on his cock while the Hammer eased out of her ass in a long slide, then drove back into her again. His testicles, warm and rough, crushed against Jed's sac, hardening to steel while Jed held off his release and savored every wickedly carnal sensation of fucking a woman together with another man.

With those provoking images pricking at his libido, Jed's cock stiffened in almost agonized urgency. Licking his lips, he restrained the sharp need to roll his hips and scrape his shaft against Velvet's belly, settling instead for a minute shift of his lower body, nestling his cock into her smooth, flat stomach.

The Hammer was behind her, his thick fingers wrapped around her small round biceps, pulling her arms back. Her breasts jutted forward, sweetly sluttish. Jed licked his lips again, wanting nothing more than to slide his hand beneath her shirt, dig one of her tits out of her bra, cup it in his hand and suck on her nipple until her breast was so sensitive to his touch that she cried out when he lashed at the dark, passion-bruised flesh with his tongue.

Jed sighed. Gray wouldn't like that. In fact, if Gray knew what he was thinking at that very moment...

Jed returned his attention to this wing companion. Gray's lips sifted through Velvet's pale hair as his eyes angled down on her head. The Hammer had it bad. Really bad. And if Jed didn't get a grip, he'd soon be in the same boat.

He pulled away from her again, knowing Gray had her firm in his grip this time. He glanced overtly at her eyes before taking a step backward, searching her expression for any further hint of interest. But it was gone. The flicker of life that had glimmered in her eyes only moments ago had been replaced with a discouragingly familiar veneer of composure.

Chapter Seven

ဆ

With his hand latched around Velvet's waist, Gray stepped out of the aero-vator. There was a hiss of compressed air just before the doors closed and the capsule rocketed off to its next destination. Gray strode across the corridor and into the Tauran tearoom. Jed followed with his sauntering stride.

Gray still didn't understand *exactly* why Jed had acted the way he had back there in the rented room. He knew for a fact that Jed was a damn good liar but it wasn't like Jed was the sort of guy who'd go to *great* lengths to avoid a fight. At any rate, whatever his reasons, the Cajun had misled Velvet, allowing her to think that the cum he'd dabbed behind her ears had come from both men, rather than from Gray alone.

Maybe the Cajun realized that Gray was out of his head over the little Adept. Maybe he was just smart enough to find the most efficient solution to the problem. Velvet hadn't wanted to wear Gray's cum, yet she had to be marked. Unaware of the fact that Gray was *trying* to cut Velvet out of the mission, Jed had probably assumed that Gray objected to her wearing *his* cum. Jed had just wanted to find a solution. After all, he had nothing to gain by whacking off into a sink.

That must be it, Gray decided, standing in the teahouse entry. He pulled Velvet into his side, fighting the urge to turn his face and run his lips across her forehead, down her cheek, over her lips, her jawline, neck, or anywhere else he could make contact. He just plain ached to rub his lips into her skin. He'd never been more aware of his mouth in his lifetime. His lips positively pricked with the need to crush, subdue and dominate.

He shifted his gaze to the woman at his side, curbing the possessive growl that rose in his chest. As long as Velvet was still part of the operation, he was relieved that she was marked and glad that it was his cum marking her. The fact was, they were already taking a bit of a chance escorting a fully clothed female into a teahouse. Polite tradition dictated she should be naked from the waist down. On the other hand, they didn't want to go unnoticed. The party's lack of taste in the matter of dress should draw plenty of attention and work in their favor.

There were no blondes amongst the Taurans. As a result, Tauran males were particularly partial to fair-haired women—when they could find them. If Velvet hadn't been marked, the teahouse patrons would have started fighting over her as soon as she'd walked through the door. As far as the Taurans were concerned, there was no such thing a free woman. All females belonged to men, existing only for a man's pleasure. But a Tauran male wouldn't touch a female when she was wearing the mark of another man. This behavior on the part of the male wasn't due to either polite courtesy or tradition. It was more of an evolutionary trait—when a female wore her male's scent, Tauran males found the scent repellant. They'd give Velvet a wide berth despite the fact that she was blonde and a damned beautiful one at that.

"You took your pain diminishers," Gray stated.

"You saw me take them," she reminded him from the side of her mouth.

"Just making sure," he muttered.

It wasn't Gray's first visit to a teahouse. And Jed had been with him the last time he'd ventured inside one, along with Jason and Matchstick. But, in keeping with his plan to attract attention wherever possible, Gray let his jaw drop as his gaze followed a Tauran female balancing a tray of tea bowls on her shoulder. He'd seen a Scarletan before but feigned astonishment at the sight of the half naked woman. Considered courtesans by some and prostitutes by those less romantically inclined, the Tauran females served up tea and sex to the teahouse customers.

A male outfitted in full Tauran formalwear stepped out of an alcove to greet them. The pleated skirt on his white peplum jacket was almost as stiff as his backbone. With a disapproving growl he took in Velvet's knee pants, his broad nose wrinkling into a snarl as he led them to a low table in a dark corner.

"What's wrong with that table?" Gray insisted belligerently, pointing out a small, square table in the middle of the room. Before their glowering host could object, Gray took off toward the table, towing Velvet along with him. Jed followed after tucking a piece of paper money into their host's lapel.

Upon stalking them back across the room, the insulted Tauran pulled the paper money from inside his jacket, ripped it in four and let the fragments float down to the table. With a snarl rumbling in his chest, he stalked away. Jed shot Gray an evil grin which Gray acknowledged with a smirk no less wicked.

When Gray lowered himself to sit on the thickly layered carpets, the tabletop hit him just below the nipples. He smiled at Velvet sitting beside him, who could have rested her chin on the black lacquered surface. Snagging a Scarletan as she passed by, he ordered three Virgin Mimis, frothed, in glass bowls.

"Virgin Mimis?" Velvet queried, her amethyst eyes wide with interest.

Jed answered before Gray could get his mouth open. "Most of the teas served here are laced with aphrodisiacs, ranging from the mildest Earth strains to the most potent Tauran infusions. Guaranteed to make you come within three minutes, with or without a woman handy." He tilted his head marginally, momentarily shifting his eyes to the long table beside them. Velvet cut a quick glance at the table then nodded her understanding.

Gray stared at the neighboring table like a visitor at an intergalactic zoo, as though he'd never seen the likes before in his lifetime. About ten Tauran males sat around the table, lapping tea from bowls, their hands in their laps. Most of them had their dicks in their fists, their penises snaking out from beneath the short, pleated skirts on their formal jackets. Their broad shoulders suggested the Taurans were members of an Educollege sports team — Destructoball players by the looks of them. One of the young men caught sight of Velvet. His face turned slowly toward her. His eyes, heavy with lust, raped her slowly while his cock turned its tusked head at the same time, its tip prodding in her direction. His nostrils flared slightly, testing the air before his gaze transferred to Gray. The Tauran bared his teeth and gave Gray a look of pure malevolent envy.

Gray's fists clenched as he glowered back at the Tauran. He reached possessively for Velvet sitting cross-legged beside him, rubbing his broad palm into her knee. He didn't like the idea of *any* man lusting after his Velvet, let alone a dictatorial ball jockey with a tusked snake for a dick. But before he could get good and truly pissed off, a long pair of naked legs passed between Gray and the offending Tauran. After the Scarletan had passed on, the Tauran's eyes followed her tattooed pussy.

Tauran females were considered among the most beautiful women in the universe, though it was rare to catch a glimpse of their faces. The women who served the tea were dressed in the strict manner required of Tauran females. A tightly fitting mask covered their faces including their mouths and eyes. Whatever the women saw, they saw from between the threads of the dark fabric covering their faces. Their straight black hair cascaded from a small, tight hole at the top of their masks. Their upper bodies were covered with intricately pleated jackets of heavy brocade. Broad bands of fabric bound their long necks and delicate wrists like wide manacles. But the pleated fabric flared broadly from the bust down to the waist, allowing the seated guests a shadowed glimpse up inside the women's heavy jackets. On their hands the women wore scarlet gloves, intricately embroidered with bright colors stitched into geometric patterns.

From the waist down, the women wore nothing other than a pair of scarlet pumps. Their nude pussies were stained with swirls of color, artistic representations of tightly curling pubic hair. The Scarletans tottered across the thick carpets on their outrageously spiked heels, their jeweled anklets clinking softly as they swayed. Some of the women wore many anklets stacked row upon row. These were the most experienced and most highly favored females. Here and there, a novice could be picked out by the small number of jeweled strings looped around her ankles.

Gray watched as the Scarletan stopped near the end of the Taurans' table. With her feet separated by one foot exactly, she folded at the waist as she lowered the tray to the table. Gray stared at her pouting pussy as she set out the fresh bowls of tea.

He heard Jed's snicker. "I think the Taurans have the right idea when it comes to women."

Gray shook his head. "I like a few curls on my pussy." He challenged Velvet with a glancing smile.

She responded by lifting his hand from her knee and dropping it into his lap. "You don't have a pussy," she reminded him, "though I'd be glad to help finance the operation should you decide to make the change."

"Thanks," he muttered, burying his irritation behind his clenched teeth. "But I don't think there's a doctor alive who has a hacksaw big enough to—"

Velvet rolled her eyes in disgust. "You're all talk."

"Actually," he returned beneath his breath, "I'm all dick."

The Scarletan, after serving out the tea bowls, moved to the head of the table and crawled onto its black polished surface. The Taurans continued their growling conversation as she waited on all fours as silently as a cat. The athlete beside her snaked a hand beneath her short jacket, squeezing a breast with one hand while stroking his dick with his other. His penis was becoming increasingly rigid as he worked his fist up and down the long, sinuous length. Gray had a clear shot of the woman's pussy. Her legs were parted and her puffy lips were damp and full.

The sight of plump, succulent pussy, ready to go, made Gray hard. Impatiently, he reached for his cock, straightening the flesh as it pulsed and thickened. He glanced at Jed. Tension marked the lines that bracketed his wing companion's mouth. With his fingers curled, Jed was dragging his knuckles over his own shaft.

The Tauran at the head of the table stood. His long penis snaked out between the pleats of his skirted jacket, ruddy and stiff. He jacked his hand down the loose skin of his cock a few times, pushing his tusks back and forth along his shaft before leaving them at the head of his dick. Then he palmed the woman's cheeks apart, spreading them open for his tusks. With his inward curving tusks holding her cheeks open, his cock darted at her like a dark serpent, in and out of her slit while he stood grunting behind her.

With drooling interest, his companions continued pumping their cocks as they watched the Tauran fuck the Scarletan. When he started to ejaculate, the head of his cock darted from the female's pussy. Curling its head, it spat milky ejaculate over her ass in small bursts, pausing to drive its head through the puddle a few times before spitting out another round of cum. When the Tauran was done, his penis gave the female's bottom a few firm smacks then curled inside the bow of the curved tusks and disappeared beneath the skirt of his jacket. The young man reached inside his jacket and produced a platinum bracelet which he held above his head for all to witness. Falling to one knee, he clasped it around the Scarletan's ankle while his companions alternately snarled, growled or grunted their approval.

The woman moved smoothly to her feet, bowing as she backed away from the table. Then she turned and tottered

94

away on her spiked heels, presumably to take a very thorough shower — she'd want to be clean for her next customer.

At this point, Gray was distracted by their own Scarletan, who served their tea in the same careful manner they had just witnessed. When the bowls of frothing tea sat before them, she crawled onto the table beside him.

Gray gave her a sharp smack on the ass. He heard Velvet gasp. From the corner of his eye, he saw her hand move instinctively for the hilt of her dagger.

When the Scarletan jumped from the table and snapped upright, he dug in his pocket and waved some paper money at her. With stiff shoulders and a haughty lift of her chin, she stalked from the table.

Velvet turned her frigid gaze on him. "You're a prick, Hammer."

He rolled his shoulders. "Just part of the act," he intoned impassively.

"You must find the role comes naturally," she returned without pause.

Gray snorted with impatience. Jeezis! Where was the woman who'd clutched at him as he'd shafted her, who'd whimpered on the end of his cock, who'd buried her nails in his ass as she came?

He leaned back on one outspread hand, pinning her with a mocking smile. "You weren't always so critical of me, Lieutenant Meadows. And I have the fingernail marks on my ass to prove it."

"Which only means I need to work on my aim. I was shooting for your balls." She curled her fingers in front of her face, glowering at them for a moment before muttering, "*Come on, claws.*"

When Jed chuckled, Gray ignored them both.

"I like a little more noise too," Gray offered up, returning to his earlier topic of conversation. "A little more moaning and panting. What about you, Jed?" He flicked his gaze at the Scarletan's back. "Have you ever...?"

The corner of Jed's mouth pulled back into a grimace. "It's like fucking a wet stump."

Velvet tilted her head. Her silken hair washed over one shoulder as she considered the Cajun. "And how would you know *that*?"

Jed lifted one bronzed eyebrow as he gave her a dark smile. "Are you sure you want me to answer that question?"

"I don't know," she countered. "How bad is it?"

"It's bad," Jed admitted without a trace of apology. "You don't wanna know everything about me."

"You don't want to know *anything* about him," Gray grunted, glad for now that the focus of attention had shifted to Jed.

He finished his tea and huffed out a sigh of dissatisfaction. "Well," he growled, palming his erection while trying to keep his gaze from drifting toward Velvet, "I don't think there's anyone here who's gotten wind of our 'escape'. We might as well leave. Try back later, maybe."

Jed turned his gaze to Velvet. "Velvet?"

She lifted her small chin. "The table at the back of the shop. Over my right shoulder."

Jed let his gaze drift over to the table she'd indicated. "Their backs are turned to us."

"They're traders," she murmured. "One of them mentioned the reward for us. He picked up the transmission early yesterday."

Gray frowned at this exchange, plowing the tip of his tongue between his teeth and biting down hard. He'd forgotten about Velvet's enhanced hearing. Jed hadn't. Damn Jed, anyhow. Gray pushed out another sigh, feeling like a dick all over again. While he'd been mooning over Velvet, fretting over her like a jealous tomcat and needling her when he got the chance, Jed had been scoring points right and left. If Gray wasn't careful, the Cajun was going to steal his woman — if only out of pure spite — right out from under his cock.

Jed crooked a dark eyebrow at Gray. "Time to make a scene?" he suggested with a faintly malicious smile.

Gray answered him with a growl of agreement. "I'm right behind you."

As Jed got to his feet and turned toward the table of Taurans, his eyes were drawn to a large party forging their way into the tearoom. The newcomers were clad in black leathers and white wraps.

Jed almost choked on his surprise.

He lowered his gaze quickly, hoping to avoid eye contact with the party of eYonans. As his gaze dropped, his eyes caught on three flat cockstones riveted into the leather crotch of a pair of tight black leather pants. He bit back a groan, fighting the urge to turn away, knowing it was too damn late. He dipped his chin and averted his face, hoping Junkie wouldn't recognize him.

That hope went up in particles when he felt strong fingers wrap around his right biceps.

"Slash," Junkie shouted. "What the fuck! I haven't seen you in years! Where the hell have you been?"

Jed chewed on the inside of his mouth. This wasn't going to be easy. But somehow he was going to have to bullshit his way past the biggest damn bullshitter ever born on the planet of eYona.

He lifted his gaze and fixed it on Junkie's fingers as though they didn't belong tucked around his arm. "I'm sorry," he muttered, "but you've mistaken me for someone else."

Never at a loss for confidence, Junkie's grip only tightened. He laughed. "I don't think so. I think I'd know Saxon's cousin if I saw him."

Alarmed, Jed's eyes widened. He couldn't help the instinctive flick of his gaze as he scanned the crowd for his cousin. Fuck! It would be hard enough to convince *Junkie* he wasn't Slash! There's no way Saxon wouldn't know him. He glared at Junkie, realizing in the same instant he'd been caught looking for his big cousin. When Junkie opened his mouth again, Jed prepared himself to yank on Junkie's long black braid and plant his fist in his face — if only to shut him up!

Help came unexpectedly from Gray. His wing companion elbowed Jed aside and placed himself squarely before the tall, rangy eYonan. "You got a problem with my friend?" he demanded, continuing before Junkie could sputter out a single word in his own defense. "Because if you got a problem with him, you got a problem with me," he growled over the group's protestations of friendship. "Spaceforce sticks together," he snarled…loud enough to reach the table at the back of the shop.

With a hand firmly clasped on Jed's elbow, Gray threw some paper money on the table then pushed him through the mob of men, between the tables and toward the teahouse entrance. Jed glanced back long enough to catch the puzzled expression on Junkie's face. A frown was on the eYonan's brow as his lips formed the words "Spaceforce". As Jed watched, Junkie grabbed at the back of Olan's leather jacket, yanking him back a step while advising the rest of his party to "forget it".

Jed shot the eYonan an apologetic smile as Gray hustled him through the door.

Twenty feet outside the teahouse door, Gray pulled up, waiting for Velvet to catch up with them. "That was handy," he said with a grin. "Those guys mistaking you for an eYonan."

"Yeah," Jed murmured, burying his hands in his pockets without looking at his wing companion.

Velvet tilted her head, her gaze moving from Jed's chin to his eyes. "eYonans aren't part of the Alliance," she mused.

"That's right," Jed muttered, forcing himself to meet her gaze. After all, she wouldn't be able to tell anything from either his chin *or* his eyes. Although eYonans didn't grow facial hair, Velvet wouldn't know whether or not he'd shaved recently. He was always careful to spend a suitable amount of time in the bathroom every dayshift, sometimes even running a lectrorazor over his face, pretending to shave.

As for his eyes? His eyes wouldn't reveal the fact that he was colorblind. And, while the inability to see in color didn't preclude anyone from joining Spaceforce, coming from eYona *did*. Jed had done his best to hide this eYonan trait from his companions, lest they started putting ideas together and figured out the truth. Jed wasn't a Cajun. He wasn't from Louisiana. He wasn't even Earther.

He was from the planet eYona.

"There aren't any eYonans in Spaceforce," Gray cut in when Velvet opened her mouth again. "And if there were, we'd be forced to report them."

Stunned, Jed's gaze ripped toward Gray.

He knew. Gray knew.

It was a staggering revelation. Jed felt as though he'd been walking around naked for the past eight years and everyone had been staring at his goods while he was the last to find out. His jaw tightened as he wondered how long his wing companion had known his secret, wondering what had given him away—*wondering if the rest of his wing were in on the secret*. But, despite the flush of heat that warmed his cheeks, he felt a deep-rooted gratitude toward his best…rival.

Gray had known that Jed wasn't Earther, yet he hadn't turned him in to Regional Command.

Gray shrugged. "Damn convenient distraction, though. It sure beat the hell out of picking a fight with that team of ball players. I think that table of traders noticed us." He grinned at Jed while Velvet finally acquiesced with a knowing smile.

Just in time too. Because at that moment, the teahouse doors opened and four very intent-looking Tauran traders paced toward the three airmen, reaching for the stunners belted beneath their pleated jackets.

Chapter Eight

ಐ

The traders' freighter was just barely big enough to spin its own gravity. And a few hours after exiting the Tauran teahouse, the lieutenants found themselves standing in one of its empty storage bays. Gray faced the freighter's thickly set captain, along with two armed amateurs. The "guards" balanced their blastukas on their shoulders, shifting them uneasily, probably wondering where to find the activation trigger. Gray snorted. Velvet could have taken them both down with nothing more than her little dress dagger.

But that wouldn't get them to Grundian High Command.

The Tauran captain scowled at Velvet, his nostrils flaring, his nose wrinkling. He turned his rancorous gaze on Gray. "Did you have to mark her?" he demanded in a rumbling snarl.

Gray gave him an offhand shrug. "It seemed like a good idea at the time."

"Just like an Earther," the captain complained to his companions, "to ruin a perfectly good blonde so that no one else can enjoy her. Earthers are a selfish breed," he grumbled.

"The males are especially bad," Velvet agreed as Gray shot her a cynical look of thanks.

The Tauran glowered at her for several seconds. "Strip!" he barked with sudden impatience. "All of you."

Gray loosened his waistband. With calm resignation, Velvet followed his lead, surrendering, without a whimper, her dagger which was tucked into the narrow sheath that was part of her waistband. Jed already had his shirt and tie off. Moments later, they stood together, the men naked except for their soft cock pockets, Velvet in a little black thong and a low-cut bra that pushed her tits together into a package that made Gray salivate. He couldn't *drag* his eyes from the small, pert perfection of her breasts. When she shivered, it was all he could do not to wrap her up in his arms.

"All the way!" the Tauran snarled.

While Gray stepped out of his cock pocket, Jed slung his at the guard across the floor. It landed at the Tauran's feet. The nervous man took an inching step away from the crumpled piece of white underwear.

"Need help with that?" Jed asked Velvet, reaching for the back of her bra as she shimmied out of her thong.

Gray's stomach clenched into a twisting knot as he watched the Cajun with Velvet. She collected her hair, pulling it in front of her shoulder while Jed worked on the tiny presslock of her brassiere. Jed's cock was erect, his hooded crown prodding into Velvet's spine, just above her ass. Gray almost ground his teeth into powder when Jed lifted his gaze and gave him an insolent smile. A moment later, Velvet's breasts bounced free as her bra slid down her arms. Gray sucked in a breath as he watched her blushing nipples stiffen in the cool air. His cock stiffened at the same time, lengthening and thickening as his hungry gaze devoured her dainty tits. His fingers curled into his palms, his fingernails cutting deep furrows into his flesh as he fought the urge to cup her breasts in one hand...and flatten Jed with the other.

An irritating scrape of noise returned his attention to the situation at hand as a narrow door opened on his left. Gray grimaced when he realized where they were going to spend the next several hours. The space they were to occupy was approximately six by three by four. Just barely enough room for the three of them—if the men bent their knees. "Hey," Gray blustered as the Tauran guards shoved them into the tight little box, "didn't anyone tell you we were important?"

Inside the cramped, narrow space, Gray and Jed faced each other with Velvet snared between their naked bodies. The Cajun spread his legs and braced his feet either side of Gray's, sliding his back down the wall a few inches. Wedged up against Velvet, Gray propped his hands on the wall either side of Jed's head. "Hope nobody's claustrophobic," he muttered, glancing down to check Velvet's face.

He heard Velvet swallow as her breasts rose. He could feel her heart beating out a nervous tattoo. Damn. If Velvet had an Achilles' heel, it would have to be tight spaces like this. Removing his hands from the wall, Gray ran his palms down her arms. "You okay?"

Her voice shimmered when she spoke. "What is this place?"

"S.I.S. Standard incarceration space," Jed told her comfortably.

"Why's it so small?"

"So they can fill it with water once a dayshift and wash everything away." Jed tipped his head backward. "The water comes in through that nozzle on the ceiling and is sucked out through a grate that opens in the floor. It works in either full gravity or zero gravity."

Her voice quavered. "They fill it with water?"

"It's only full for a few seconds," Jed soothed, "then it starts emptying. In between, you hold your breath."

A small ridge formed between Velvet's brows. Her pearly white teeth nipped at the plump pad of her bottom lip. But her words were stronger this time when she spoke. "You sound...awfully damn comfortable about the whole situation."

"I've been incarcerated a few times," Jed allowed easily. "Gray?"

"I've been incarcerated a few more times than that," Gray admitted in a growl.

"Might as well get comfortable," Jed encouraged her in a quiet voice, pulling her back against his chest.

Gray fought the urge to bare his teeth and snarl. His fingers tightened on Velvet's arms. His first primal male instinct was to clutch her away from Jed. He squelched the impulse but only with an immense amount of effort. Jealousy and animosity wasn't going to help. Things were bad enough. He didn't want to increase the tension in the small enclosed space. It must have been a little like this at Etiens—a little like this but a lot worse. Close and tight, bodies crammed together like fish in a barrel, the air sharp with the sweat of fear, while the pounding explosions cracked the walls and sent the reinforced ceiling crushing down in heavy chunks.

At least it was quiet in the S.I.S. And they had a little light glowing down on them from a tiny square panel on the wall.

Forcing himself to a low simmer, Gray took a deep breath and continued stroking Velvet's arms. He forced a smile onto his features while continuing to palm the silken flesh that rounded out her shoulders. "Hey, Cajun," he murmured. "I don't think we've ever been in a *tighter* situation."

Jed snickered. "You're forgetting Suzie Gates."

Gray pushed out a soft sigh of frustration. Damn Jed, anyhow. "She was tight," he admitted reluctantly.

"Suzie Gates?" Velvet murmured.

"Long story," Gray muttered evasively.

"Longer trip," Jed added with an unabashed laugh. "It's surprising what two men will resort to when they're stranded in space for three months...with only one woman between them."

Gray ignored him. Jeezis, Jed could be a dick sometimes.

Stroking down to Velvet's wrists, Gray lifted her small hands and pulled them to his waist. Jed had coaxed her head back on his shoulder and Gray watched her face while sliding his hands up and down her hips. Her bright, unique scent filled the small space. Pressed up so close against her, Gray couldn't help but get harder as he watched her from beneath his downcast lashes. Jed's face was right beside hers, his mouth nuzzled up against her ear. When Jed caught Gray's gaze, the cheeky bastard gave him slow smile. Gray ground his teeth. The Cajun was thinking about the same thing he was. Sex.

"Close your eyes," Jed encouraged the girl gruffly. "Ignore the hard-on," he added.

"Whose?" she asked in a trembling voice, "yours or Gray's?"

"Gray's," he chuckled. "Why do you think I told you to close your eyes?"

In the next instant, Velvet's eyes flew wide as the thin light that filtered down from above flickered. A second later it died, leaving them in utter darkness.

Velvet stifled a small cry. Instinctively Gray pulled her toward him while Jed's deep voice murmured quiet reassurances. Gray's hands slipped over her shoulders and rounded her breasts as he leaned over her, running his lips down the side of her face, searching for her mouth.

Velvet averted her face but soon discovered she had nowhere to go. Jed's face on her left cut off any escape in that direction. Gray's lips below her right ear, hemmed her in on the other side. Trapped between the two men, Velvet had no choice but to accept the caress of Gray's lips below her ear, on her neck and along her jawline while Jed continued to soothe her with his deep, murmuring voice.

Gray crept up on her in slow degrees, brushing his lips over her chin, feeding his breath across her cheek before finding her mouth and encouraging her to relax with the warm nudge of his lips. His heated breath mixed with hers as his mouth sifted across her parted lips. Almost stoically, she accepted the brush of his lips without any further struggle, yielding to the tentative probe of his tongue. True, her body was taut with tension and her kisses lacked a certain degree of passion but…

Gray repositioned his mouth over hers. It felt so good to be close to her, he could almost thank the Taurans for stuffing them into the box together. He longed to talk to her, to apologize, to explain his actions and tell her how he felt about her. But crowded into a narrow closet with another man hardly seemed the time to tell a woman you loved her.

His cock surged and stiffened as he palmed her breasts. Jeezis, she felt good. She tasted good, her flavor crystalline, her tongue tangling with his as he explored the silken, inner recesses of her mouth. The silence grew heavier as his cock thickened. He couldn't help wanting her. All he could do was hold her and pretend they were alone together. And with the lights out, it was black enough to carry off the pretense—for a while.

Jed chuckled softly in the darkness, interrupting the quiet spell of intimacy.

Reluctantly, Gray pulled his lips away from the warm envelope of Velvet's mouth. He closed his lips on her bottom lip, sucking at the sweet fleshy pad before dragging it through his teeth. "What?" he growled at Jed.

"I was just thinking," Jed answered.

"About?"

Again Jed snorted out a soft sound of amusement. "The look on the commander's face when you told him you were in love. Command must have thought you were nuts."

Gray stiffened. Beneath his hands, he felt Velvet holding her breath, waiting for his reaction.

"Is that what you were going for?" Jed prodded him. "Were you trying to bail on the mission?"

Gray shook his head in the darkness. "Fuck you, Cajun."

Jed laughed. "Why'd you say it then?"

Briefly, Gray wondered what Jed was hoping to achieve with this line of questioning. It was so hard to tell with Jed. Not only was he a brilliant liar, the Cajun was damn deceptive, not to mention manipulative when he wanted to be.

Suddenly, Gray didn't care what Jed's motives were. Jed had just given him the opening he needed. "Because I meant it," Gray answered quietly.

Several seconds of silence followed. But he felt a change in Velvet. Her cool stiffness turned to acceptance as her body relaxed beneath his hands. His hands continued to move gently over her breasts as his breath roughened to an aching rush that hurt his chest. She sighed against his mouth and he heard the Cajun expel a long, soughing breath at almost the same time. Velvet melted between them, arching slightly into Gray's hands. When he moved his hands down to her hips and slid them around her backside, he found Jed's hands already there, cupping her bottom in long sweeping caresses. Growling, Gray forced his hands inside Jed's palms, pulling Velvet into his groin, nestling his shaft into the soft curls on her mound — hard cock to sweetly cushioned pussy.

"Relax, Gray." The Cajun put his hands on Velvet's waist and pulled her back again. On the back of his hands, Gray could feel the hard ridge of Jed's cock questing for her ass. The tight skin wrapping Jed's erection was hot and damp as it dragged against Gray's knuckles.

Gray didn't like the idea of Jed's naked cock that close to his skin. With a snort of frustration, he moved his hands back to Velvet's hips as he rocked against her, knowing that he was driving her backside into Jed's groin. As he strained against her, the breathing in the tiny space became harsher, more hurried. It soon became obvious to everyone in the cell that this wasn't going to stop short of climax.

Velvet smeared her slender body up against Gray's. Her breasts were warm where they touched his chest, her mound damp where it pressed into his erection, questing for contact. Instinctively he crushed into her, squeezing her against his wing companion as he groaned in frustration.

Jed's voice was soft. "Take it easy, Hammer. This isn't going to be like Suzie. I'm just going to hold her for you."

Gray nodded in the darkness — telling himself that would be all right — that it *had* to be all right, because at this point he couldn't stop himself. But when he felt for Velvet's breasts again, he found that the Cajun had beaten him to the prize. Jed's hands were beneath her tits, lifting them. Gray would have objected except he didn't seem to have much to complain about. Tipping his head forward, he suckled her breasts while Jed fed them into his mouth. Jed's thumbnail slid across the smooth washboard of Gray's teeth as he stroked Velvet's nipples into tight knots. Gray's mouth closed around Jed's thumb as his tongue lashed at her nipples whenever the Cajun gave him an opening.

At this point, Gray was suffering from both acute need and overwhelming jealousy, wondering what the fuck Jed was doing with his cock — and his mouth for that matter. But the Cajun spoke just then, urging Velvet to move her legs apart. At that point, Gray could have kissed him.

The next thing he knew, Jed was lifting her legs and Gray was stroking the outside of her naked thighs as she braced her feet against the wall behind him. "Wider," Jed whispered. When Velvet shifted her feet on the wall, her lips parted along the line of his shaft. Gray could feel the delicious damp heat of her open pussy pressing against the ridge of his cock.

He wished he could get a look at the puffy pink paradise kissing his cock. He regretted, now, that he'd rushed at her the first time they were together but, Jeezis, he'd been hot. Licking his fingers, Gray worked them down between their bodies and got them on her pussy.

Jeezis Skies, women were so fucking delicate, soft and warm. So hot. So wet. So vulnerable. Such a sweet fragile place to claim with the brutal thrust of your cock.

The lips of her sex were slightly parted and Gray played the pads of his fingertips over the pout of her labia, exploring every micro-meter of her outer lips before going on. He held his breath as he opened her with his fingers and touched her tender inner sex for the first time. Together they gasped quietly as Gray dragged his fingertip across the silken folds tucked inside her plump pussy lips. A little more careful exploring yielded the tight little knot of her clitoris and he sighed as he teased it with a light touch. She was rolling her hips slightly before he went on, reaching low into her sex and dragging his finger up to her clitoris again.

He slid his fingers down through her pussy until his fingers sank into the wet opening of her vagina. His fingers brushed against Jed's and he realized the Cajun had his hands beneath her bottom, pulling her cheeks open, running his own fingers close to her entrance, skidding on the moisture that slipped from her tender opening.

"She's wet," Jed murmured in the darkness. "Are you going to play around all day, or are you gonna get in there and fuck her?"

Gray breathed out a light snort of frustration. Damn Jed, anyhow. The guy had no finesse. You didn't fuck a woman like Velvet. You made love to her.

Even if you *did* want to bang the ass off her.

"Yeah," Velvet murmured in a cool breath that washed across his ear, "you going to play around all day or what?"

Oh, Jeezis. The girl was asking for it.

And he was just the man to give it to her.

Gray levered his cock downward, slipping the head through her delicate folds and claiming the tender notch of her sex, flexing his knees and forging upward, filling her. She took in more of him this time. Apparently, her body was already adjusting to accommodate the full length of his cock. And though she wasn't quite as tight as she had been the first time, her cunt hugged his cock as though it was *made* for his dick. It excited Gray to think that, given time, he'd be able to sink into her all the way to his balls. With his hands on her hips, he pulled her up as he retracted his shaft, then forced her down to meet each driving thrust as he rode into her. His eyes strained in the darkness and he wished for a little light so he could watch his thick root gleaming with her juices.

As if in answer to his prayer, the lights flickered, filled the tiny room, turned back off, then on again.

Immediately, Gray lowered his gaze to his cock where he stretched the puffy pink flesh that surrounded her vagina. He groaned as he pulled his hips and watched his shank forge forward to stretch her wide again. Panting out short, raw breaths, he checked her face and found her eyes closed, her expression unsettlingly devoid of anything that could truly be called passion.

Jed's green gaze was hard and glazed, fixed on Gray's face. His legs were spread wide, his knees slightly bent as he held Velvet's cheeks open and slotted his cock along the crease of her ass.

Gray fed Velvet's soft pussy, filling her with cock, holding off his own need to climax, awaiting some sort of sign from her, some sort of surrender, by word or action—a few murmuring sighs, a whimper of pleasure. Something that would tell him she was ready. But she wasn't giving up any secrets other than those revealed by her body. Although he was packed in her tight little piece, he was sliding easily, his cock coated with her sweet sex juices.

Gritting his teeth, determined to feel her come before he spent himself inside her, Gray pounded her back against the Cajun as the air filled with rasping male grunts. As he banged into her with controlled intensity, he felt her inner muscles seize on him, clasping him in a series of shuddering spasms. He shafted her deeply, plowing right to the back of her cunt, stilling to experience the pleasure of her hot sheath quivering around his cock. He watched her face for an admission of emotion but she was lost in the orgasm, staring upward as she arched against Jed.

With a harsh burst of sound, Jed's voice intruded into his lust-fogged mind. "Gray!" he choked out, his strained laughter edged with desperation, "don't stop now!"

Gray expelled a savage snort. He resumed the grinding thrust of his hips, watching Jed's eyes. They were unfocused with pleasure as Gray drove Velvet's bottom against Jed's cock. With every driving thrust that Gray delivered, Velvet's ass was crushed against Jed's groin, chafing at the shaft caught between her cheeks. A few slamming thrusts later and Jed was grunting as his cum pumped out into the cleft of her ass. Gray was shouting at the same time, ejaculating in blistering surges as Velvet came again, her contracting vagina tightening along his length as she milked him dry.

"Oh man," Jed panted a moment later, skimming his lips along the elegant curve of Velvet's jaw. "Good thing we're not in zero gravity or we'd be swimming in cum." With his eyes closed, the Cajun smiled as his lips moved. "I'm glad you two made up," he mumbled on a yawn.

Gray grunted. In retrospect, Jed's motives seemed a little clearer now. He'd maneuvered the two lovers back together…so he could get off himself? "That worked out pretty well for you, didn't it, Cajun?"

Jed shrugged. "It could have been better," he murmured. His head tilted slightly and his eyes cracked to reveal a thin seam of green light. "You gonna let me in next time, Velvet? Seems a waste to leave your dark little buttonhole clenching on air."

Velvet closed her eyes and smiled as though she was considering the idea and didn't find it altogether distasteful.

Gray growled a rough breath into her ear. "Just let me know if you get hungry, sweetheart. After I kill him, we can eat him."

Despite this outward display of machismo, Gray sighed inwardly on an unnamed sense of dissatisfaction. It wasn't the same. It definitely wasn't the same as what they'd shared up against the door in Velvet's room. The coupling they'd just experienced was great sex, gritty and satisfying. But the helpless feminine surrender just wasn't there. Something was

111

missing. She'd never lost control. She'd orgasmed twice — no doubt about that. But they were...controlled orgasms.

If sex were a game of conquest, then Gray suspected that Velvet had just swept the board and passed go — twice. She'd just had sex without involving her emotions, which was just about the same thing Gray had been doing for all these years. Before he met Velvet.

Damn. Gray didn't know what the fuck to think.

Maybe it was just Jed's presence that had Velvet holding back. Either that...or the way Gray had shattered the girl's trust. Gray didn't like the prickles of guilt that followed on the heels of this idea, so he didn't spend much time on it. Ruthlessly, he shoved it to the back of his mind.

He gazed at his two companions. Jed's eyes were closed, the back of his head tilted against the wall, his temple resting against Velvet's forehead. Velvet's face was slightly turned, her lips almost touching Jed's neck. Her eyes were closed as well, apparently in sleep, her breathing even and shallow. If Gray had been an artist, he would have considered the picture romantically intimate. As a layman, he thought it could have been improved dramatically by the removal of Jed.

The air was close in the tight space, filled with the sweet, lusty scent of shared sex — hard male heat and soft female warmth blended in dark proportions. Reaching down to straighten his sated shaft, Gray pressed his wet cock into the slight swell of Velvet's belly and repositioned his knee between her legs. It was hard to find a comfortable way to share the tiny space but that wasn't why he'd moved his leg. He'd moved it because he wanted his knee pressed against the heat of her pussy. He wanted to feel her warm pulse against the hard muscles above his knee. Her thick, tender sex was hot where it rested against his leg, oozing a warm trickle of cum onto his thigh, their mixed juices slipping from her sheath and joining with Jed's cum as it dripped through her crease.

Velvet shifted in her sleep, rubbing her pussy into his thigh. Their combined scents smelled unexpectedly good to him—an erotic blend of sex and satisfaction.

"It wasn't the same, was it?" Jed murmured.

Gray narrowed his gaze on Jed, not exactly happy to hear the Cajun voicing his own recent doubts. The Cajun's eyes were closed and Gray decided to ignore him.

But Jed wouldn't let it go. "It wasn't the same as before," Jed repeated in a drawl. Finally his eyes opened into their customary narrow slits, revealing a thin glow of green light. "Part of her has…withdrawn," he stated. "It probably started at Etiens."

Gray grunted his understanding, those prickles of guilt revisiting with a vengeance. Velvet had as much as told him in her room that she'd been reluctant to form relationships since Etiens. Yet, despite that fact, she'd let him in. She'd let him into her body and more, yielding beneath him as together they had shared the most intimate coupling he'd ever experienced. They'd *shared* it. Of that he was certain.

She had opened up for him. Opened her heart. Opened everything. And he'd shut her down again with that stupid camera stunt. At least, that was what Jed was implying.

Fuck.

"She still has plenty of spunk and fire," Gray argued halfheartedly.

"That isn't the part that has withdrawn," Jed informed him quietly.

"Whatever," Gray growled.

Jed continued, apparently dissatisfied with what he must have considered Gray's cavalier response. "She's an Adept," he articulated, "try to imagine how efficiently she might do that."

Great! Gray hadn't just fucked up. He'd done a damn efficient job of it. He'd fucked up completely. At this point, the prickles were having a fucking field day, jabbing away at his conscience like armed demons. "You said yourself that she smiles in target practice."

"Yeah. When she's blowing something up. That doesn't exactly count."

"What are you trying to tell me?" Gray grunted, lifting his arm and rubbing his damp brow into his biceps.

Jed locked his gaze on Gray's. "It will probably take both of us to bring her back."

Ah. There it was. There was Jed's motive. Damn sneaky Cajuns. You never could trust them, even when they *were* from eYona.

Gray growled, his eyes shifting back and forth as he searched Jed's somnolent gaze, not really understanding how this might be true while somehow fearing that the Cajun might be right. It *hadn't* been the same. She *was* holding back. On top of that, she'd wanted Jed to mark her, rather than Gray. Velvet had her shields up where Gray was concerned. And as Jed had pointed out, when an Adept put her shields up, she probably did a damn efficient job of it. A mere human heartfelt apology and profession of love probably wasn't going to bring them down again, at least not any time soon. At this point, Velvet might see Jed as a safe zone, somewhere she could go to shelter her heart. Jed hadn't done anything to harm her, while carefully building her regard for him.

"Maybe," Gray conceded with a growl, hoping the exchange was over. Did Jed *have* to make him feel like absolute shit? Fortunately for him, Jed changed the topic with his next words.

"How'd you know?" Jed asked him quietly. "How'd you know I was eYonan?"

Gray snorted softly. The note of gratitude in Jed's voice had him questioning Jed's motives yet again. Perhaps the Cajun's actions were somewhat altruistic, after all. Maybe the Cajun was just trying to help Velvet. Maybe he was even trying to help Gray when he maneuvered them back together.

After all, Jed did *owe* him. Gray could have turned him in to Command a year ago.

Gray grunted, "Suzie Gates."

Jed groaned. "Suzie knows?" he whispered. "Fucking O! If Suzie knows, everyone knows!"

Gray shook his head. "Suzie doesn't know. No way. If she did, you wouldn't be on the Force anymore. I don't think anyone knows, though you should probably tell Jason and Match so they can...cover for you."

"How'd *you* know?"

Gray lifted one shoulder. "Couple of things gave you away. First, the way you...shared a woman. You did it a lot more comfortably than an Earther would."

"Multi-relationships aren't that unusual on eYona," he admitted. "My father has two wives. What else?"

Gray growled, the sound almost scraping with reluctance. "You never had any stubble. Not even at the end of the shift. There, when all three of us were going at it—you, me and Suzie—there were times when your face was...pretty close to mine." Gray snorted. "I almost mistook you for Suzie once, your skin was so smooth. I almost kissed you once!"

Jed stared at him. "No shit?"

Gray growled, "Tell anyone and you're dead."

Jed smiled, knowing how much the idea would bother Gray, knowing that the confession would be hard for him to make and that the admission itself was a turning point between the two men—a moment of male bonding. It prompted him to start making his own confessions. "I...always wanted to join the Spaceforce," he began but Gray cut him off.

"I know," Gray told him. "You don't have to explain to me. Spaceforce is lucky to have you. I hope eYona is admitted to the Alliance one day."

"Thanks," Jed mumbled without looking at him. There was a certain amount of relief in finally sharing his secret and knowing that at least one other man agreed that what he was doing wasn't so wrong.

"I'll tell you something else," Gray volunteered. "I don't believe the eYonans are hiding the Grundians—not knowingly."

"Not knowingly," Jed agreed, a note of worry in his voice. If eYona were somehow implicated with the Grundians and if his secret were discovered...then that bridge would be burning when it finally came time to cross the damn thing.

Velvet shifted her head and the men fell silent as she nuzzled her cheek against Jed's collarbone. A wave of tender emotion settled Jed's concerns for the time being as he smiled down on her. "I wish I could see her the way you do," he murmured, "with all the variations, all the...colors. Are her eyes...like mine?" he asked with an unexpected twinge of longing, knowing that the reason some eyes were dark and others were light was because they were different colors. But the whole concept of color was difficult for him to grasp. He wasn't even certain his question made sense.

Gray smiled. "No," he told him in a gruff whisper. "Yours are green, like...grass shoots. Mine are gray like a cloudy day. Hers are...amethyst."

"Amethyst," Jed breathed out a quiet sigh, knowing amethyst only as a dark crystalline rock. The color that it represented was a treasure he could never hope to fully appreciate. "How many hours do you think we'll be in here?"

Gray shook his head.

Jed hesitated before he spoke. "Because the way you've got this planned...the pain diminishers might wear off before we even get to the Grundians."

Gray gave him a nod. "I know," he said quietly. "But you know as well as I do that Command is *counting* on us spilling our guts."

Jed nodded. They hadn't been told anything Command didn't want the Grundians to know. "The sooner we talk, the better for everyone."

"That's right," Gray answered. "But we can't seem too eager to talk or they'll smell a trap. We'll have to string our captors along for a while."

Jed grinned. "I can do that. I've had plenty of experience—"

"Yeah. Yeah. Quit bragging, you obnoxious ass. We're talking about Grundians, not women."

Chapter Nine

ဆ

The Main Inquisitor of the Grundian High Command drew a long, slender finger down the length of his nose. The overhead lights gleamed along his gilded nails. His nostrils quivered as he sniffed sharply. A thin platinum circlet gleamed on his brow, translating his Grundian thoughts into Earther and delivering them to his lips. "What *have* you three been up to?" he drawled with a smirk.

Gray ignored the Grundian. After spending approximately seven hours in the freighter's S.I.S., they'd been transferred to a Grundian military space station where they now faced the Main Inquisitor. They'd reached Grundian High Command and met the mission's objective. Match and Jason would be currently situated a safe distance from the space station — about twenty-four hours away at a scale of one:twenty — in order to avoid the Grundian's sensor sweeps. By now, his wing companions would have transmitted their coordinates back to Earth Base Ten.

The Tauran traders had fed them and permitted them to dress before removing them from the freighter but the S.I.S. had never initiated its cleansing cycle and Velvet remained marked by both men after their sweaty tryst in the tiny cell.

Gray was relieved the trio hadn't been split up after being transferred to the space station but wondered why their new hosts had required the men to strip again while allowing Velvet to retain her clothing. Even more disconcerting was the chain cinched around his neck. Too small to pass over his head, the sliding choke chain could, however, be drawn tighter. The chain-link collar was fastened to a heavy leash of the same material which disappeared into a hole at the outside edge of a circular stone floor. Jed was similarly chained on the other side of the arena while Velvet was shackled to the floor with an iron manacle clasped tightly around her booted ankle. A five-foot length of chain fixed to the center of the floor allowed her to move inside a ten-foot arc. Opaque walls curved into a dome over their heads.

The Inquisitor stood well outside the arena behind an instrumented podium. His long, diaphanous tunic was slit up the sides all the way to his waist. Its frilled hem brushed a floor of polished metal patterned with squares and rectangles. Beneath the long gauzy garment, a pair of brilliantly white and obscenely tight leggings covered his legs and hips. As the Grundian fingered the controls on the panel set into the top of the pedestal, Gray made silent plans to strangle the man should he be careless enough to come within reach of his chains.

"I smell both of you on the female," the Inquisitor commented, drawing another long breath in through his nose. He brushed his straight white hair back behind his shoulder. Blue veins snaked across the pale, translucent skin of his face. His irises alternated red and blue with every beat of his heart. "But I'm guessing you're the predominant male," he said, extending a long finger in Gray's direction. "At least, it's your cum that I scent dripping from her pussy." He turned his disapproving gaze on Jed. "What did *you* do? Jack off on her ass?"

While Gray growled, Jed just returned the Inquisitor a self-indulgent smirk.

"Just like an Earther," the Grundian grumbled, his small rosebud of a mouth pursing in disapproval, "no sense of decorum." He pushed out a melodramatic sigh. "Are you wondering why your female is still clothed while the two of you are naked?"

Gray feigned disinterest, unwilling to concede any curiosity on the point.

"I thought it would be entertaining to watch you two rip her clothes off. Entertaining…as well as arousing."

Gray cleared his throat. "Why would we do that?"

The Inquisitor rolled his eyes. "So that you can fuck her, naturally. *Honestly*! Earthers are *so* dense."

Velvet spoke up smoothly. "I'll be more than happy to remove my clothes right now should you think it necessary."

The Inquisitor rested his hands on his hips and pouted. "Well, aren't *you* a little spoilsport!"

"No sense ruining a perfectly good Spaceforce uniform," she pointed out.

Gray didn't miss Jed's proud smile. Chipped ice and diamonds all the way. He shook his head as they shared a grin together.

"Right," the Inquisitor announced, dusting his hands together. "Let's get down to business. Tell me everything you know about the Velvet Hammer."

The blank silence that ensued seemed to please the Grundian to no end. The fact that he was pleased made Gray uneasy.

"During our attack of Earth Base Ten, we picked up an interesting communication trail that passed between your two ships."

Velvet snorted softly. "You call that an attack? The only thing you managed to hit was your own ships."

The Inquisitor's pulsating eyes narrowed on her an instant before giving Gray a keen look. "She's mouthy, isn't she?"

"You don't know the half of it," Gray muttered.

"Will she tell me about the Velvet Hammer?"

"She probably would," he answered, "*if* she knew what you were talking about. In that case, you probably wouldn't be able to shut her up. The problem is, we *don't* know what you're talking about. After your attack at Earth Base Ten, we were arrested for a communications infraction. Normally a communications infraction isn't a big deal. But for some

120

reason, Command was pissed as hell. They seemed to think we knew something we weren't supposed to know. Whatever it was, it was huge. After we escaped, we ran like hell."

The Grundian hit two buttons on the control panel, playing aloud the same communications file Gray had heard back on Earth Base Ten.

"Cajun? Do you have Velvet? Hammer out."

"She's here."

"If you fuck with her, you're dead."

"Acknowledged. Cajun out."

"How do you explain that?" the Inquisitor asked.

"Explain what?"

"Don't act dumb with me, Lieutenant."

"What makes you think it's an act?" Velvet incised with clear-cut cynicism.

The Inquisitor ignored her. "I want to know everything you know about the weapon referred to as the Velvet Hammer."

"The Velvet—" Gray laughed. "There's a weapon called the Velvet Hammer?" He grinned across the room at Jed. "No wonder Command was angry. Let me explain. I was looking for Lieutenant Meadows. Her name is Velvet. My name—my nickname—is Hammer."

"Your name is Graham Hamm."

"Yeah but my nickname—"

"Never mind," the Inquisitor cut him off with a wave of his finely molded hand. "I'm not interested in either your name or your explanation. Tell me everything you know about the weapon being developed on Earth Base Ten."

"I'm trying to *tell* you. We don't know anything about the weapon."

The Grundian sighed as he targeted Gray with his flickering gaze. "Maybe I'll just take your hand, one finger at a

121

time," he drawled with a lazy smile. His tilted his head in Velvet's direction. "Do you think your female will miss them?"

Gray had to give the girl credit. Velvet didn't even blink. Her expression was that of utter disinterest. Maybe that was because she wasn't *acting*. Quite possibly, she didn't care if Gray lost his fingers.

"Let me have a dagger and I'll give you a hand—*his hand*," she told the Grundian with chilling dispassion.

"Thanks," Gray sniped at her.

The Grundian laughed at this exchange. "I'm tempted to let you have at him, believe me. But you're an Earther. *And* an airman. I know a little bit about the females on your Spaceforce. You'd try to kill me first no matter how much you hated him. Am I right?"

"Not this time," Velvet told him very convincingly.

He laughed again as he shook his head. "What did he do to you?"

Velvet's expression was glazed with a thin coat of brittle hardness.

"Did the big handsome bully break your heart?"

Her voice was light, her tone flippant. "I don't have a heart," she told the Grundian. "Anymore," she growled in an aside to Gray.

"Good," drawled the Inquisitor. "I won't waste my time trying to cut it out, then."

He grinned when Gray blanched. "Does the idea bother you, Earthman?"

Gray threw back his shoulders and announced, "You'll have to kill me before you can get to her, Sir."

"How noble," Velvet cut at him beneath her breath.

"Yes, how noble," the Inquisitor echoed with a chuckle. "But fortunately for you, we'll be forgoing torture and amputation as well as murder during the inquisition."

As if on cue, a door slid open. An aide, robed in flowing chiffon and wearing a translation circlet, stepped through the opening. On his outstretched palm, he balanced a sterile tray. A stainless steel injection pistol sat in the middle of the tray.

Involuntarily, Gray flinched.

The Grundian chuckled. "But we *do* have ways of making you talk."

Gray felt a yank on his neck as the Inquisitor pressed a button. His chain whipped into the hole at the edge of the arena. Seconds later, Gray was on his knees beside the hole. A few more seconds and his face lay pressed against the cold stone floor, the slack in his chain reduced to nil. On the other side of the arena, Jed had been forced to the floor in the same manner.

"We've been vaccinated against truth serums," Gray warned the Inquisitor.

With a sinister smile, the Grundian lifted one carefully plucked eyebrow. "This is something a little bit different and much more pleasant...for us at any rate."

He flipped a switch on the console and the dome that enclosed the arena lit up to reveal stadium seating ringing the circular hall. As Gray watched, Grundian spectators threaded up the ramps and along the aisles, chatting with friends while locating their seats. At least Gray assumed they were chatting. Their mouths were moving. But no sound penetrated the thick, transparent walls.

The Main Inquisitor gazed around at the rising seats then addressed his aide, "We'll leave the sound off, shall we?"

The aide gave him a confirming nod.

As the Inquisitor's assistant floated onto the stone floor, Gray's attention was transferred from the crowd to the aide with the tray. He eyed the injection gun with halting distaste. "What is it?"

"Something new we've been experimenting with," answered the Inquisitor. "Let's just call it an anti-inhibitor."

From the other side of the arena, he heard Jed snort. "A lust amplifier."

"What do you mean?" Gray demanded.

"It's an aphrodisiac concentrate," Jed explained in a voice like gravel. "No doubt a Tauran product. After we're injected, we'll be horny enough to fuck a wall."

Gray struggled to make eye contact with his wing companion. "How's that going to make us talk?"

As the aide approached Jed with the gun in hand, the Cajun's gaze slipped to Velvet. "With the right inducement, we'll go mad with need. Eventually, we'll do anything, say anything, in return for a little ass."

"Which means?" Gray plied him.

"Which means you might as well apologize now for what you're going to do to Velvet."

The aide pushed the nose of the pistol against Jed's arm. A quick click followed as the tiny needle injected the concentrate into his biceps. Jed scrambled to his knees after the Inquisitor fed him several feet of chain. "I'm sorry," Jed told Velvet as his chin jerked upward and his head dropped back on his thickly corded neck. His eyes closed a moment then reopened. A glittering sheen hardened his liquid green eyes. His cock, already thick with healthy interest, now throbbed and surged and stiffened as Gray watched. It was unnatural. Jed's cock bulged and purpled before his eyes.

Jed shook his head in resignation as he raped Velvet's body with his eyes. "Listen, sweetheart," he managed to croak out between large, rough breaths. "Do everything you can to prepare yourself. To get yourself wet. Everywhere." His face twisted with effort. "Do you understand?"

Velvet gave him a quick, businesslike nod that was at odds with her expression. The pearly edge of her teeth was buried in her bottom lip.

Watching her, Gray experienced an overwhelming surge of dread mixed with panic. "Don't hurt her," he roared at Jed.

But Jed was already across the arena, tearing at her clothing. With both hands bunched in her shirt, Jed ripped at the thin olive fabric. It came apart with a harsh tearing noise.

Gray's eyes cut from Velvet and Jed to the aide who approached him with the injection gun. Gray was almost overwhelmed with the terrifying idea that life as he knew it was about to end. If he had been facing his death, there was one thing he'd want to be certain that Velvet knew. "Velvet," he shouted, "remember what I told Jed in the S.I.S. No matter what happens, no matter what I do. I meant what I said!" Gray strained to avoid the approaching aide, scraping several square inches of skin from his shoulder and leaving it on the stone floor—but the next thing he felt was a small sting in his biceps and the next thing he experienced was utter madness.

The Inquisitor fed him some chain and seconds later, Gray's hand was in Velvet's panties, tearing them away from her dainty ass while Jed ripped them from her tufted mound. Velvet tried to help them get her clothes off but they never gave her a chance. Then both men tried to climb on her at the same time and all three of them went down in a tangle of flailing limbs and rattling chains.

Gray didn't fight Jed. He wasn't trying to take the girl away from Jed. He was just trying to take the girl, period. He was *stinging* with arousal—one huge, burning hard-on from the ends of his hair to the soles of his feet. He wasn't the least bit interested in what Jed did or where he was. Gray had only one concern. Getting fucked. Nothing else mattered. As long as Jed didn't directly interfere with that objective, he was safe. They were two men with one woman. But there were three places to fuck a woman. Any of those three locations would do. Gray wasn't picky—just horny enough to kill himself rutting.

About the time that they got Velvet on her knees between them, their captor shortened their chains. With his finger tapping at the control panel, the Inquisitor sent the metal leashes slithering into the holes at the perimeter of the circle, yanking both men away from her. The links around Gray's neck tightened as he tried to fight his way back to Velvet, his eyes glued to the promise of carnal paradise tucked between her beckoning thighs.

Velvet scrambled to her feet just out of reach of the two slavering men. Dressed in nothing but a pair of brown leather boots and the olive drab tie that hung limply between her breasts, she turned in a slow circle, her quiet gaze assessing first Gray's face, then Jed's.

The Inquisitor laughed contentedly. "You can start talking whenever you want," he drawled lazily. "The sooner you talk. The sooner you get the female."

Jed snarled as he threw himself at Velvet. The metal links tightened around his neck, biting into his flesh, crushing his windpipe and darkening his face.

Velvet leapt toward him. "No, Jed!" she shouted, pushing him backward to give him some slack in the collar's chain, reaching up to loosen the links cutting into his neck. But he wouldn't even let her do that. He wouldn't even let her save his life. As she reached for the collar, he clamped his hands on her shoulders and forced her to her knees. With one hand wrapped around the back of her skull, he dragged his cock head down to her mouth and thrust the streaming head between her lips. But Velvet must have managed to back him up at least a few inches before he plowed his cock down her throat, because his face lightened a bit as circulation returned to his neck.

Oblivious to his own discomfort, Jed threw his hips at her face.

"Does that bother you?" the Inquisitor asked Gray. "Watching your companion fuck your female's mouth? Or can you only think of that unfilled pussy, sitting wastefully empty?"

Gray threw himself against his bonds. The links around his neck tightened and he whimpered like a dog on a chain. As he watched, Jed's chain sank into the floor, dragging Jed away from Velvet. The Cajun's cock popped out of her mouth, shining and wet, coated with his own pre-cum as well as her saliva.

The Inquisitor gave Gray a nod as he pushed a button, releasing a few feet of Gray's chain. "Your turn."

Gray fell on her like an animal. He grabbed her by the neck, his thumb pressed against her nape, his fingers wrapping her throat as he forced her face against the floor and drove into the slit between her legs. Velvet bit back a sharp grunt as Gray slammed into her, his steel-hard shaft scraping at the barely damp walls of her channel. After two or three thrusts, the Inquisitor shortened his chain again, yanking him away from Velvet. His knees scraped against the stone floor as he tried to claw his way back to her.

Like two rabid dogs, the two men fought to reach Velvet, strangling themselves on the heavy links circling their necks. Velvet scrambled to her knees, her expression wary as she viewed her recent companions as a new and dangerous threat.

"Prepare yourself," Jed almost strangled himself to remind her.

Velvet nodded, licking her fingers quickly then sliding them between her legs. With her knees spread and braced on the floor she rubbed her mound and fingered her clit.

The Inquisitor's expression was languid as he watched Velvet's fingers in her pussy. Beneath his long gossamer robes, his flat nipples pulsed pink and purple as his blood coursed through his veins. "Tell me about the Velvet Hammer."

When no answer was forthcoming, the Inquisitor reset the controls, giving them a few slack inches of chain. The men gasped in a few lungfuls of air. But air was only their secondary concern. Their eyes remained glued on Velvet as they writhed within their bonds and strained toward her.

"Tell me about the Velvet Hammer and you can fuck the woman all day long."

Gray nodded his greedy assent while Jed warned him with a snarl.

"It's a passive weapon," Gray panted, ignoring his friend. "They're developing it at Earth Base Ten."

The Inquisitor played out a few inches of Gray's chain. On his hands and knees, Gray crawled across the floor toward Velvet. She inched toward him, reaching him before he could choke himself. Like an animal, he licked her pussy, lapping hungrily at her plump outer lips.

"When will it be ready?" the Grundian demanded.

When Gray didn't answer, the Inquisitor allowed Jed to move a step toward Velvet. "When will it be ready?" he asked again with slow precision.

Gray shook his damp hair out of his eyes. "I don't know," he shouted. "We don't know!"

"Ten months," Jed lied.

With this misrepresentation, Jed was permitted to take another step closer to his goal.

"He's lying!" Gray roared. "He doesn't know. He doesn't know any more than I do!"

Jed curled his lip and bared his teeth in a grimacing smirk.

"Tell me about the weapon," the Grundian demanded in a slow, silky drawl.

Gray swiped his tongue over his lips, collecting Velvet's taste into his mouth. A thin whining sound rattled in his throat. He needed more than the taste of her pussy on his lips. He needed her cunt wrapped around his cock. "It will incapacitate all those of your race without having any effect on Earthers."

"Incapacitate?"

"It's a nonviolent explosion. It will...put you to sleep or something. I don't know!"

"What is its range, duration?"

Gray tried to think his way through the dark lust that clogged his mind. "Twenty hours. Twenty hours within its sphere of influence."

"What is its sphere of influence?"

Gray eyed Jed jealously. "I don't know."

The lie rolled off Jed's lips as easily as breathing. "Thirteen planetary measures."

Gray howled as Jed crept toward Velvet. "Liar! He's fucking lying!" Gray shouldered the spittle from his chin as he strained on the end of his chain.

"Well, if *he's lying*, why don't *you* tell me the *truth*," the Inquisitor invited him. "Perhaps you need further inducement?" He motioned toward his aide who approached Gray again, gun in hand.

Gray's muscles knotted and rippled, boiling beneath his skin as he fought his chains. He was already eaten alive with need. He'd penetrated Velvet before her body was ready for him. He'd *felt* her channel fight his entry and he'd plunged ahead anyway, slamming his cock to the back of her vagina, smashing into her cervix.

According to his own rough code of chivalry, he'd already committed rape. What the fuck would a second dose of the anti-inhibitor do to him?

Rape and manslaughter?

As a Spaceforce lieutenant, his first obligation was to protect the Alliance. Even in his current condition, with the drug skewing his reasoning all to hell, this knowledge hovered at the back of his mind. But above all of this rose his need to protect Velvet. He was already acting like an animal. What if a second dose reduced him to a *dangerous* animal? What if he could no longer protect Velvet—from himself? What if he destroyed Velvet trying to get to her? A man his size could easily break a woman in two. Break her back. Break her neck.

He bared his teeth and snarled. Protect her. Fuck her. Love her. It was all a tangle in his head. In his current state, he couldn't separate the three ideas. Emotions, compulsions, needs—everything was a knotted jumble of confusion. Everything hurt—his head, his heart, his cock. It felt as though his dick might explode into tattered ribbons if he didn't get inside a woman. He wanted to howl with anger and frustration. Instead he whimpered with need.

He panted at the end of his chain, his body screaming for release, his mind churning toward a decision while lust humped through his bloodstream like an evil destiny. He was damned if he did—but he might be a whole hell of a lot more damned if he didn't. Finally he broke, though tears of frustration and helplessness streamed down his face. "You want to know the truth, asshole? Here's the truth."

"Gray!" Velvet shouted. "No!"

Gray ignored her, his voice raw with anguish and defiance as he bared his teeth and snarled, "You've been set up, you prick. You wrote your own death sentence when you picked us up! The Alliance has a tracer beam on me. They knew we'd end up at your High Command. An alpha-class cruiser is on its way to this location as we speak. When it gets here forty-eight hours from now, this place is going up in particles!"

The Inquisitor cut a keen gaze at his aide.

"Their craft was searched," the aide replied, his expression doubtful. He waved the gun in the air, a few inches away from Gray's arm. "There were no transmitters, no beacons on their ships. We made certain of that before the Tauran freighter left Delta Base Twenty. We asked the traders to bring the Hexapods with them, then searched the ships again when they arrived here."

"It's in me!" Gray screamed in utter panic, eyeing the injection gun that hovered near his arm. "There *is* no transmitter beacon. They're sweeping space for me. It's in my blood. They injected me. Ions in an unnatural combination. Scan my blood for an iron and copper molecule."

The Inquisitor pulled a handheld scanner from a cradle on the panel and threw it to his aide. Lowering the gun in one hand, the aide waved the scanner at Gray with the other then grunted as he read the output on the scanner's tiny display matrix. He stepped away from Gray and carried the instrument to his superior.

The Inquisitor's brows rose as he glanced at the output reader in his aide's hand. "It appears you're telling the truth."

Gray went limp with relief. "Now, let me fuck her," he growled.

"Which means your friend was lying."

Gray snorted out a snarl of victory as he glared at Jed. "Let me fuck her!" he shouted.

"He'll have to be punished," the Inquisitor proclaimed with sly cruelty.

Gray nodded, his eyes greedily locked on Velvet's pussy as he strained toward her.

The Grundian gave Gray a conspiratorial wink. "We'll shorten his chain and let him watch you take your reward — see how much he can take before he goes absolutely out of his mind." The Inquisitor stabbed a button on his console and sent Jed's chain rattling into the hole on the floor.

The Cajun went to his knees, gagging as the chain dragged him backward. He scorched Gray with a look of hateful scorn. "It didn't take much to get you to spill your guts," he spat at Gray. "Just a little pussy."

"*Fuck* you, Cajun! I told Command I'd spill for her."

"You said you'd spill to *protect* her, you fucking hypocrite."

"I *am* protecting her," Gray cried.

A soft chuckle sounded behind Gray. Seething with fury, he cut a vicious glance backward at the Grundian.

"Earthers are so melodramatic," the Inquisitor snorted. "And they are so remarkably attached to their females." The

Grundian sighed comfortably as he addressed his aide. "We have forty-odd hours before their alpha-class battle cruiser gets here. When it does, we'll be long gone. In the meantime, I love watching Earthmen mate. They're so...*earthy*. All that grunting and sweating and thrusting. It's so...primitive. Put in the order to change location to be executed in three hours. We'll head for space sector Epsilon, scale of one:thirty."

The aide saluted then flicked a finger at the captives. "We'll space these three before we leave?"

The Inquisitor laughed as he flipped a switch on the control panel. From out of the patterned metal floor rose four blocks of steel. When they clicked into place, the shining blocks formed a throne-like chair. "No," he answered, picking up a remote and throwing himself into the metal chair. "We'll leave them here in one of their gunships. When the Force does their sensor sweep, they'll find their officers *right* where they expect them to be. Right *here*. The Alliance will assume their officers are still onstation and that *we're* still here with them!"

Gray was only vaguely aware of this exchange. His mouth was watering as he watched Velvet's pussy. Saliva trickled down his chin. Pre-cum streamed from the slit in his cock head and slicked the head of his shaft. He licked his lips and swallowed several times.

The Inquisitor pushed a button on the remote, loosening Gray's chain. He charged toward Velvet, grabbing her ass up into the air as he turned her and slammed into her cunt. There were choking sounds from Jed as he tried to reach her at the same time, strangling inside the tightening clamp of his collar. But Gray didn't care about Jed. He just kept crushing into Velvet. With his fingers clawing at the cheeks of her ass, he held her in position, hardly aware that she was moving with every pounding thrust, inching toward Jed, dragging him along behind her.

He was finally fucking her. Nothing else mattered. Nothing in the universe.

Except for her voice.

"Gray," she urged as he pounded into her. "Help me reach Jed. He's choking."

"I don't care," Gray snarled.

"Yes, you do," she argued gently. "Help me, Gray."

He pulled her cheeks wide, watching her tiny opening, the delicate pink skin stretched thin and tight as she took his cock. Oh, God. He was fucking her. He was fucking her sweet, tight, hot little cunt. "Why the hell should I?"

"Because he's Spaceforce. He's your wing companion."

"I don't care about Jed!" he roared, sweat dripping from his chin and pattering down onto her ass.

"Then do it for me, Gray. Do it for me," she coaxed.

Gray growled, gnashing his teeth like a dog.

"Do it because you love me, Gray."

"I love you." The words grated from between his clenched teeth as he tested them on his lips. He continued slamming into her, thrashing her pussy, flogging her with his cock. "I love you," he gritted a little more certainly. He might be stark, barking mad but he could still recognize the truth of those three words. In a world gone mad those words seemed his final link to sanity. He took comfort in their familiarity. He took refuge and solace in their strength. If he knew nothing else in the universe, he knew that he loved Velvet Meadows. Lifting his gaze from her finely molded ass, he transferred it to Jed's purple face. Slowly he inched forward as his own collar tightened.

When Velvet reached Jed, she didn't waste time trying to help with his collar. Instead, she clamped her mouth over his cock. At that point a minor miracle took place. Somehow, for some unknown reason, it occurred to Gray to reach out and loosen the metal chain embedded in Jed's corded neck.

Jed slumped, grabbing at Gray's shoulders as Gray steadied him. Their eyes connected and held. Jed thanking Gray with his eyes. Gray reassuring him with his own expression. Together the men shared a silent communication wherein they both simultaneously received and granted forgiveness.

Then Jed's eyes closed as he came in Velvet's mouth.

Attacked from before and behind, Velvet grunted as she serviced both men. With a stiffening groan, Gray grabbed and held, grinding his hips against her ass as he emptied inside her cunt.

There were a few panting seconds of sanity before it started all over again.

Gray heard the Inquisitor's voice behind him. "That was entertaining. Let's muzzle the female this time."

Jed groaned. "Velvet. Did you swallow everything?" he asked desperately. "Spit it out. Spit it into my hand."

"Too late," she muttered, wiping her mouth on the back of her hand just before the aide slipped a barred mask over her face.

Jed started to pump his dick, spreading his legs wide. "Don't let me enter her," he rasped at Gray. "After I come, use my semen to lubricate her." And in the end, Gray had to intercede as Jed lost control and attempted to take her ass. Gray finished him off. With his fingers wrapped round Jed's cock, Gray pistoned his fist over Jed's shaft, forcing the Cajun to come on her derriere.

As the Cajun spilled out over her skin, Gray slid his fingers through Jed's thick, slippery cum, moving it swiftly to the tight kiss of her ass. By that time, he was losing hold of his own tenuous self-restraint. His fingers shook as he plunged his slick fingers through the tight ring of muscle. Collecting more of Jed's cum, he painted it around the rim of her puckered entrance.

Before Gray had finished, Jed had her tie in his fist, yanking her up to her feet. He flexed his knees. With his shaft in his hand, he thrust between her legs, jerking his hips upward, trying to seat his cock inside her pussy. "No," Gray insisted with strained chivalry. "You take her ass. You'll do less damage."

And that was the last of chivalry for a long time.

The two men fought and grasped and tangled. Jed couldn't give her much time to adjust to the male girth stretching her anus. With several brutal lunges, he forced his way inside her, filling her ass, while Gray fucked her cunt with a savage powering rhythm. Gray came before Jed had forged his length all the way in. And after Jed did finally come, he didn't bother to withdraw. He just stayed inside her until he thickened again moments later.

* * * * *

Several orgasms later, the air was slick with the musky scent of sex. Both men were painted with sweat while cum streamed down their legs in burning rivulets. Gray's feet were braced wide on the slippery stone floor. The pain diminishers he'd taken approximately fourteen hours earlier were no longer contributing any relief. His legs trembled with strain as he cried out in agonized ecstasy, his cock rubbed almost raw but still building and spewing and coming in a wash of savage, painful pleasure. Jed was muttering eYonan curses as his body convulsed and his hips jerked in violent spasms. His eyes closed as he came for perhaps the tenth time and he sagged against Velvet, almost going to his knees before Gray caught him.

Gray wrapped his strong fingers around Jed's biceps, momentarily halting his fall. Apparently at the limit of his endurance, Jed continued to slide downward. With a curse, Gray grasped at the drooping man, his fingers spread wide and clutching at Jed's ass. With his fingers hooked beneath Jed's buttocks, he hefted him upward a few inches and clamped him into place. With Velvet trapped between them, Gray started ejaculating again.

Through it all, Velvet gritted her teeth, moving the men forward a few inches then backward again, trying to keep them both alive and breathing while they simultaneously tried to kill her with sex. But somewhere in the intervening hours, her body must have started adapting because, in the midst of the brutality, she started coming. At this point, the hard edge of the aphrodisiac was beginning to wear off. Gray's eyes connected with Jed's. The two men shared a brief exhausted moment of relief as Velvet clenched around their cocks, her body shuddering as she climaxed.

Jed's brown hair hung over his shining brow in twisting wet ribbons. His forehead fell forward, resting on Gray's shoulder as they stood panting together. The poor bastard moaned as he tried to lift his head. Gray gave his ass a hitch upward. He could feel Jed's breath, hot and rushed, like liquid fire, washing over his collarbone. He looked down on Velvet's head. Her face was turned, her damp cheek plastered against his slick chest.

Jed tried to lift his head again.

"It's okay, Jed." Gray reset his fingers, tightening his hold on Jed's butt. Tilting his own head, he rubbed his temple into Jed's damp hair. "It's okay."

"Is it over?" Jed groaned.

"Not for me," Gray rasped. "I'm coming at least one more time."

"Velvet?"

Her voice was muffled but hearteningly indignant. "I'm just getting started!"

Jed gave an exhausted laugh, rubbing his eyes into Gray's wet shoulder.

A twisted grunt drew Gray's eyes to the throne-like chair behind him. The Main Inquisitor had swept his robe aside and unbuttoned the flap on the front of his tight leggings. His legs were spread wide as he played with his pale cock and stroked his own balls. His transparent penis thickened and Gray watched his cum shoot up his length then spill out on his smooth, flat belly.

Gray snorted with disgust as he eyed first the Inquisitor then the audience. "Decorum, my ass," he muttered.

He shook a few sodden strands of ink-dark hair from his eyes and started moving his hips again, his hands and arms binding both Jed and Velvet to him. His vision was overlain with a haze of exhaustion as he braced his legs for what he hoped was the final drive. He was almost asleep on his feet the next time he came, staggering to support Velvet's weight along with most of Jed's.

In the next instant he gasped as a stinging blast of frigid water hit him. The Grundian aide had turned a hose on them, shocking them apart as though they were a pair of randy dogs fucking a bitch in heat. Gray tumbled to his knees and took the freezing bolt of water in the chest. It clobbered him like an icy fist, smashed into his face then moved on to slash at his companions.

Gray slumped to the floor. As his eyes closed in defeated exhaustion, he pawed around on the cold wet stone, reaching for Velvet. He found her leg, her hip, her arm. When he found her small hand, he wrapped it up in his fist.

The last thing he heard before he tumbled into sleep was the Inquisitor's harshly musical laughter. It was with a trace of melancholy that Gray realized that he'd never heard Velvet laugh.

Chapter Ten

ഇ

Gray was floating in a sea of cum, drifting aimlessly. The sensation was pleasant, the situation unlikely, which meant he was probably asleep. Damn. He needed to be awake. He was sure of it. There was something important he had to do, though he couldn't for the life of him think what it was. He was certain, however, that he needed to wake up and do it.

In his dream, he forced his eyes open and looked around. If he could believe his eyes, he was on a Grundian space station. A long-legged Scarletan wrestled with a huge, tusked penis as long as a fire hose. As it ejaculated, the thick flow of cum surged toward him in slow motion.

That couldn't be right. He must still be asleep. He had to wake up. All he needed was the right motivation. Something that would startle the pants right off him. Some appalling idea like the end of the universe...or Jed stealing his woman.

That worked. Gray woke with a start.

He was floating in his Hexapod. The craft was in go clear mode. He found himself surrounded by the utter blackness of space rolled in a glittering sprinkle of tiny white stars. On the other side of the cabin, Jed floated near the command seats. Velvet drifted a few feet above him, her head touching one of the ships star-bedecked walls.

He and Jed were still naked. Small beads of water drifted through the cabin. But Velvet's hair had dried since the dousing they'd received onboard the Grundian space station. Thick strands of silken sunshine floated around her face like independent entities. Her crumpled tie stretched away from her neck like a ragged banner. The muzzle that barred her mouth seemed a harsh contrast to her delicately curling lips.

One of her boots floated on the other side of the cabin, leaving one foot uncovered. Gray frowned at her slim ankle. It didn't...look quite right.

His eyes narrowed in speculation as he rubbed a hand over his rough growth of beard. Evidently, the whole time her foot had been manacled, Velvet must have been trying to work her foot out of the boot. The bones in her ankles had either shifted or shrunk during the time she was chained. Eventually, she would have been able to pull her foot right out of that damn manacle. She might have even been able to take out the Inquisitor and free her two wing companions. Although, how much good that would have done with half the ship watching in the stands...

Gray shrugged then pushed out a heavy sigh of relief. They were alive. That was the main thing. The Grundians hadn't spaced them.

That was the good news. The bad news was that they might have blown the mission. If the alpha cruiser was still on its way to their location, it was coming to the wrong place. Feeling spent right down to the bone but knowing he had to act, Gray twisted his head groggily. When he had his bearings, he pushed off toward the controls. Moments later Jed followed, swimming through the air and dragging himself into the second command seat.

"We're drifting," Gray muttered as he belted himself into his seat. As his body made contact with the chair, the control panel came to life and filled the small cabin with light.

Jed's voice was flat as his fingers ran over the control panel above his head. "Perspective drive is inoperative. Weapons are down."

"Do a full systems scan," Gray ordered.

"Environmental functions are out," Jed informed him.

Gray's heart stumbled. More bad news. "Reboot," he ordered more calmly than he felt.

Jed entered a string of commands and flipped a switch. "It's mechanical," he reported a moment later. "The bastards sabotaged our oxygen supply system."

"Matchstick will find us," he returned confidently. "He'll have a read on our coordinates. They'll find us."

Jed spun his seat around and regarded Gray quietly. Dark shadows beneath his narrowed eyes marked his exhaustion. "Yeah, they'll find us...about sixteen hours after our oxygen runs out."

Gray shrugged as he flipped switches and systematically reviewed the output. "They might already be on their way here."

"Their orders were to remain a safe distance from the space station."

Gray snorted gamely. "Since when did Match or Jason ever follow orders?" Jabbing at a button on the arm of his chair, he opened a communications trail. "This is the Hammer looking for a Matchstick," he said, slipping into an ancient communication lingo used by the team to confuse potential eavesdroppers. "Come back, Match."

The next few seconds of silence were long ones. Velvet floated into the space between the two chairs, anchoring herself with a hand on each of their shoulders. Gray turned his darkly stubbled chin and brushed his lips over her fingers. "Are you okay?" he murmured, searching her face.

She gave him a superior little smirk as her tie floated toward his eyes. "I don't know how to tell you this, Lieutenant but I imagine I'm a tad better off than *either* of you guys."

Gray lifted a hand and resituated her tie behind her neck. Her Adept traits had probably helped her body to cope, both during and after their ordeal, aiding her to heal quickly. At this point, he felt like he could use a little Adept blood himself. It felt as though somebody had skinned his cock and used it to roast marshmallows.

140

"The commander was right," he told her. "Your Adept traits came in handy after all."

"That's hardly surprising," she answered as she reached back and worked at the mask that covered her mouth. "What *is* surprising is that your infatuation came in handy…after all."

Infatuation? Gray pushed out a tired sigh. "It isn't infatuation," he told her quietly. "I love you…and that's the only reason Jed is still alive."

The speaker crackled. "Matchstick here. How ya doin', Gray?"

"Alpha Tango, Match. You still have a read on us?" Gray watched as Jed helped Velvet loosen the muzzle. When she pulled it from her face, it floated away across the cabin.

"Ten-four, good buddy. We're reading you like a beacon."

"We're no longer in the company of the Grundians. Repeat. The Grundian space station has departed this location."

"Understood, Hammer. Command anticipated this contingency. In fact, the Grundian space station is presently headed straight for hell."

That, at least, was good news. Gray did some quick figuring. "Command assumed we'd spill everything, including our cover story?"

"That was the plan, Gray. They told you everything they wanted the Grundians to know. Not everything you were told was factual, however. The Grundians didn't have forty-eight hours. They had considerably less time. To make matters worse, the Grundians took off in exactly the wrong direction. Our battle cruiser departed from a rendezvous point in space sector *Epsilon*. At the rate of speed which the Grundians are closing with our cruiser, apocalypse is anticipated in approximately twenty hours."

"Space sector Epsilon!"

"Ten-four. You heard me right, good buddy. eYona gave them safe harbor."

Gray glanced at Jed. Together they shared a wry smile. "Understood," Gray returned. "How is Spaceforce tracking the Grundians now that I'm no longer onstation?"

There was the sound of a throat clearing. "Ah, Gray? I assume you left a little something behind."

"I didn't leave any blood on board," Gray returned.

There was a snort of amusement from Matchstick. "The tracer elements that were in your blood? Gray, they were in your semen as well."

Gray smiled grimly. "Understood, Matchstick. What's your ten-twenty?"

"Fourteen hours off your sunboard bow. Hurtling toward you at top speed. We started heading your way as soon as you reached the space station, after we'd transmitted the coordinates to Command."

Gray grimaced. "Match. Our environmental functions are out."

A short silence followed. When Matchstick continued, his voice faltered. "Understood. Understood, Hammer. How long do we have?"

"Eight hours," he stated quietly. "We'll take steps to conserve."

"We'll squeeze something extra out of these machines," Match told him. "Hold on, guys. We'll get there."

Gray slumped back in his chair, drooping with a bone-weary exhaustion that crept into every muscle on his body. His smile was grim as he planted his feet on the floor and swiveled his seat to face Jed. "I don't suppose you'd consider spacing yourself?"

Jed barked out a short laugh. "So you can live happily ever after with Velvet? Not a chance. We're in this together. All the way to the end."

"What if we named our first child after you?"

"Forget it."

"You're a selfish bastard, Cajun."

"I've already done the calculations," Jed answered with a tired smile. "With the amount of oxygen left in the Hex, two airmen wouldn't survive any better than three."

Gray shifted his gaze to Velvet. "What about *one*?"

Velvet snorted. "Don't you two go getting all heroic on me. You can't space yourselves without my help."

Jed put his fingers together in a steeple. "There'd be at least a small chance of one of us surviving."

"Yeah," Velvet growled. "One survivor. One inquest into your deaths. One airman out of the Spaceforce on a charge of murdering her companions. *One airman reviled throughout history*. No thanks," she stated with cool efficiency.

Gray considered her quietly for several seconds before checking Jed's eyes. Was Jed thinking what he was thinking? There was a good chance Velvet would live whether they spaced themselves or not. She was an Adept. The change in the cabin's atmosphere would be gradual, probably gradual enough that her body would adjust to the diminishing levels of oxygen. As usual, Jed's gaze revealed nothing.

Finally, Gray gave her an accepting nod. "Okay, Lieutenant," he said softly, ignoring the melancholy that crept into his soul like a cold wraith. Velvet would probably live. With that idea to sustain him, he could face his own end.

But he didn't have to be fucking happy about it.

Velvet would probably accept his death without a single tear—brave and emotionless to the end. He should have been glad he was sparing her from grief. Nonetheless, he somehow wished that she'd mourn him. He sighed. If the girl was bereft of emotions, he had no one to blame but himself. "We'll have to reduce our activity to a minimum. Lie low."

Jed shook his head. "It won't be enough. It won't be nearly enough. It'll take them fourteen hours to get here. We'll be out of oxygen in eight." His exhausted gaze drifted to Velvet as he let his head drop back onto the command seat's headrest. "I'd rather wear myself out and die in my sleep. Whaddya say, sweetheart?"

Gray cut in before she could voice her response. "You can die in your sleep if you want to but you can forget about wearing yourself out on Velvet."

A muscle ticced in Jed's jaw as his eyes narrowed to green slits. "Why don't we ask Velvet what *she* wants?"

Gray hedged. He didn't want to know what Velvet wanted. If he had to die, he wanted to die thinking he was somehow special to her. Not just one of two men she was willing to fuck. "Forget it," he snarled. "I'm not sharing her again. I'm not sharing her...willingly. Back there with the Grundians, we didn't have a choice. Now we do. I'm *not* sharing her!"

Jed snorted impatiently. "What difference does it make? You'll be dead in a few hours! *I'll* be dead in a few hours!"

Gray turned and pinned Velvet with his gaze. "I'd do anything for her," he told Jed. "Anything but share her again."

"You'd do anything for her? Then why don't you let her tell us what *she* wants?"

Gray swallowed hard, shaking his head as he faced Velvet. "You're going to have to choose between us. Jed or me."

She said nothing. She gazed serenely back at him as though unaware of the emotions that were raging between the two men. He wanted to grab her by the shoulders and shake her. He wanted to rail at her. *Are you fucking blind? Can you not see what you mean to me? What you mean to us?*

He wanted to cry because he'd done this to her.

Reaching for her hands, he cupped them in the open shell of his fingers, rubbing his thumb into her palm. "I know Jed has never hurt you, Velvet. But he'll never love you as much as I do." Setting his jaw, he challenged the Cajun with his gaze.

Jed's expression was defiant though he blinked several times. "Whatever, Gray. I don't know how much you love her. I just know I'll never love anyone more."

Velvet cleared her throat. "I'm sorry, Gray," she started.

Gray's heart fell. Whatever it was Velvet was sorry for, he didn't want to hear it.

"By the Princess!" Jed exploded, falling into an eYonan accent for the first time in the eight years Gray had known him. "We've only a few hours left and you're wasting them arguing! Can you not see what you're doing to her? Are you *trying* to make her withdraw? Are you *trying* to make her close up entirely? Why the hell does she have to choose?"

Gray shouted, "Is that all you can think of? Getting fucked again before you go?" Glaring at his wing companion, Gray braced himself for Jed's reaction, certain there would be one, either verbal or physical. Possibly both. Violent and ferocious. Instead Gray witnessed something he never thought he'd see in his lifetime—the Cajun choked up over a woman.

Jed's voice cracked as his eyes darted to the floor. "I just...want what you want, Gray. I just want a chance to...make up for what happened back there on the space station." His voice was rough with emotion. "I've...never even *kissed* her, Gray."

Beyond exhausted, Jed covered his face with his hand. He was used up to within an *nth* of his being. On top of that, his stomach churned in tight dizzying waves of nausea. He was a hard bastard—tough—and everybody knew it. He liked sharing women with other men. He'd shared Suzie with Gray and he'd been willing to share Velvet with Gray. But not like that. Not like two animals raging over a piece of ass. Not as though Velvet were nothing more than a cheap fuck.

He wasn't like Gray. Gray was wing leader. Decisive. Sure. Gray had probably never experienced a moment's doubt in his lifetime. When Gray fucked up, he shrugged it off and carried on—corrected it if he could, got over it if he couldn't. Jed drew in a shaky breath, wishing he had that sort of strength. But he didn't. He needed this. He needed this opportunity to wash away his sins, the chance to set things right. A thick lump of emotion rose in his throat when he thought about what Velvet had done back on the space station. How she'd dragged Gray across the stone floor to get to him—on her hands and knees—to save his life. The idea...almost crippled him. If he weren't about to die anyhow, it was an image that would haunt him for the rest of his life.

He didn't want to fuck Velvet. He wanted to make love to her. He wanted to kiss her clit and taste her release as it coated his tongue. He wanted to kiss her *lips* for Skies' Sake! He wanted her on his cock, wrapped up in her wet heat, waiting for her first fluttering contraction, savoring her last clenching spasm before he exploded inside her. His cock was beaten and battered and bruised but it still pulsed with a thick, urgent, driving need for this final mating.

For several seconds, Gray watched the Cajun staring at the floor. Jed's head was bowed, the fingers of one hand splayed across his forehead, his palm shielding his eyes. Gray shook his head. It wasn't pleasant watching a man—one of his wing companions and a damn strong one at that—reduced to his lowest common denominator. Gray couldn't help but feel sorry for his wing companion. In Jed, Gray saw his own sorry-ass weakness for this woman. Unlike Jed, he was just too proud and too stubborn to let it show.

Damn! It was just so hard to accept the idea that Velvet might love Jed more than she loved him. Or as much. Or even almost as much. "Fuck," Gray muttered on a growling sigh. He was a dick. And if he wasn't careful, he was going to die a dick—instead of the leader he was supposed to be. They had a matter of hours left. Jed was right. It was stupid to spend them arguing.

Releasing his restraints, he pulled himself over to Jed's chair and wrapped an arm around the back of his shoulders. "Jed," he argued softly, "you don't have anything to make up for. What happened at that space station was just…part of a mission. These things happen when you're Spaceforce. You did what you had to do—we all did what we had to do! But somehow, through it all, *you* managed to keep Velvet at the forefront of your mind. While I was screaming, 'let me fuck the bitch', *you* were reminding her to prepare herself. You…you did *good*," he murmured in a rough baritone.

Jed shook his head. "You never called her a bitch," he mumbled from behind the screen of his hand.

"You know what I mean. You did good," Gray told him as he flicked his gaze at Velvet. "Didn't he, Velvet?"

Gray caught Velvet's shielded expression and almost groaned. As if Velvet could help! Miss Chipped Ice and Diamonds! Fuck. While Velvet was an emotional cripple, Jed's emotions were about to cripple him. Gray's companions were blinking out like black stars and he was the only source of gravity within a thousand planetary measures.

But there was still time and a way to fix this—and Gray knew it. He tugged Jed into his side and gave his shoulder a rough squeeze as he smiled at Velvet and cleared his throat. "Come back," he said quietly.

Velvet tilted her head. She looked like a porcelain doll—a beautiful, still, emotionless doll. "What do you mean, Gray?"

He rolled his shoulders as he struggled to explain. "After what happened to you at Etiens, you withdrew. You closed up to protect your heart and your emotions from future loss. Because you're an Adept, you did it far more efficiently and completely than a human would. But when we were together in your room, you opened up for me. Something…incredible happened that night. Something I've never experienced before.

I'm in love with you, Velvet. And I think that—for a very short span of time—you felt the same way about me."

He checked her face and she nodded solemnly.

"I know I fucked up that night with the camera. That was bad. But that's not the worst part..." He stopped to collect himself. "Since that night, you've withdrawn even further, deeper. That's my fault."

When she didn't argue, he forged ahead, "For your own sake, you need to forgive me. You need to understand that I didn't mean to hurt you. I didn't think you were a slut. I didn't think you were a bitch. I just thought..." Gray faltered, struggling to express himself.

"He thought you were tough," Jed mumbled, finally lifting his face out of his hand. "He thought you were strong, like one of us—like me or Match or Jason."

"Or Bellamy Anders," Gray suggested.

Jed sniffed back a ragged chuckle. "Nobody's that tough."

"Probably not," Gray conceded with a crooked smile.

"He just thought you could take it," Jed summarized.

"And I was right," Gray followed up softly. "Despite everything you'd been through, you *were* tough. When you marched into the mess hall the next morning, spitting fire from all chutes, I knew I was in trouble. I've never been more afraid," he said. "I've never been more proud," he added quietly. "And I've never been more in love...than at that moment."

Both men watched her. Both men held their breath.

Velvet's tentative smile was almost shy. "You thought I was tough?"

Gray expelled a long breath and smiled. "Yeah."

"There she is," Jed murmured at his side.

Gray turned to look at him.

"There she is," he said simply.

Gray frowned, his gaze traveling from Jed back to Velvet. Something had changed, though he couldn't put his finger on exactly what was different. Whatever it was, Jed saw it clearly. He, on the other hand, only saw that Velvet didn't look quite so…remote.

Jed's mouth hooked up into a wry smile as he pushed out a dramatic sigh. "Ah, shit. You two go ahead and have fun. Don't mind me. I'll just sit here and jack off on my own."

Gray made a face at him. The bastard was being noble again. Damn Jed, anyhow. The guy could out-noble the Nefarian Regent's mother.

There was a muffled snort from Velvet.

Gray snapped his head around to stare at her. She was laughing. Deep chuckling giggles fell from her mouth like a brilliant stream of joy. Her teeth gleamed, pearly white in her wide grin. Jeezis. She had dimples. Two of them. For several moments he gaped, his mouth hanging open in wonder. She was laughing and it was the most beautiful damn thing he'd ever seen. He followed her gaze to Jed.

Gray rolled his eyes as he tightened his grip on Jed's shoulder. "Aw, come on then." He grinned at the Cajun. "Let's go wear ourselves out. What do you say, Velvet?"

Chapter Eleven

ହେ

It was as though a switch had been tripped in Velvet's heart. One minute it was in the off position, the next minute it was on. As she watched the two men put aside their rivalries and jealousies in a bid to bring down the barricades guarding her heart, it was as if tendrils of emotion slowly unfurled around her heart and reached carefully toward them.

Except for extremely brief intervals, she'd been missing a heart ever since day forty-two of the blitz at Etiens. It was damn empty, drifting through life without a heart. No doubt a 'droid felt more than she did. It might be an effective way to stay alive but other than that it didn't have much to recommend it.

She'd felt a flickering shift of emotion that first time she'd seen Gray in the mess hall, then lost the elusive feeling almost as quickly as it had come. Like a mirage, it had shimmied away as she watched him walk toward his friends. The sensation was akin to grasping at the tail end of a dream, feeling it slipping away, not quite remembering the dream but certain that it represented the ultimate nirvana.

It sprang to life again when Gray came to her room—as he sat beside her, flipping through her sketches. When he'd dropped her notebook and kissed her, she'd snatched at him, clung to him, spread her legs gratefully, feeling her heart open at the same time. When the dorm super had ordered him out of her room, she could have cried, scared to death that her feelings would leave with him—that love and caring and tenderness would walk out the door when he did. But they hadn't. For one perfect night, she'd fallen asleep with her emotions tucked warmly around her.

They'd shut down again when she'd found that camera the next morning, though. They'd gone into lockdown. At that point, she'd thought she'd never forgive Lieutenant Graham Hamm.

The next time she'd felt remotely human had been in the small bathroom on Delta Base Twenty, as Jed had dabbed cum behind her ears—gently, caringly—turning an awkward situation into a deeply tender moment, drawing his fingers along her jawline as though he was bestowing upon her skin the finest Nefarian perfume.

Jed.

Right from the start, with gentle care and unfaltering determination, he'd chipped away at the block of ice that had encased her soul, even when it meant pushing her into Gray's arms instead of pulling her into his own. It was Gray who had started her back that night in her dorm room. But it was Jed who had made sure she got there.

How could she fail to love both men?

Her heart ached as she looked at them. They were so handsome. Gray, so strong and confident—like a rock. Jed, aloof and somehow vulnerable despite the mask of indifference he insisted on wearing, as though every day he put his heart on the line and nobody was ever there to take note of his sacrifice.

Gray was never vulnerable, not for a moment—not even when he'd announced to his entire Command that he was in love. His cheeks had burned ruddy with heat, dark with defiance. Gray was sure of himself. Certain of his love.

Just as certain as Velvet was that she loved both men.

"I want you both," Velvet told them. Her voice trembled with emotion and a wonderful frisson of excitement. She felt deliciously alive, pulsing with passion, love, tenderness and an urgent burning need. She wanted to make love to her lovers, to take their strong masculine flavor into her mouth. She wanted to know again the taste of Gray's ravenous mouth and experience for the first time Jed's hungry kisses. She yearned for his tongue taking her mouth possessively. She wanted to lick the cum from his cock as it surged over his skin and coated the length of his shaft, savoring its salty tang before swallowing it. She wanted to suck Gray off and compare their flavors, certain that she'd find them equally delicious. She wanted to feel Jed's rough fingers gliding over her breasts, plucking at her taut nipples while Gray took her vagina, his thick shank stretching the rim of her vulva.

"How do you want to do this?" Jed asked Gray, a tight edge of tension riding his words. A black shadow cut across the dark beauty of his skin, casting his rugged features into relief as he released himself from the command seat bindings and lifted away from the chair. His cock sprang taut against his belly, a thick luscious stretch of male flesh, wide at the root, swollen at the head, dark with arousal and the abuse it had endured back at the space station.

"Let's move to the sleeping compartment," Gray answered, his voice thick and rugged, a masculine mixture of sexual tension and soul-scraping emotion. "We can free-float for now but later on one of us will want to anchor themselves."

"What do you want, Velvet?" Jed asked. "What do you want first?"

Velvet's murmured answer was soft with longing, her skin moist with a fine sheen of sweat, a tortured ache building beneath her belly. "I want to kiss you...both of you. But...I don't see how that's going to work."

"Oh, baby," he muttered, reeling her against his chest so that her nipples grazed against his own smooth skin. "We'll make it work."

"We'll need a lubestick," Gray rasped and Velvet shivered at the promise of those words, the prospect and anticipation that accompanied their intent. Gray was referring to a lubricating stick—to ease his entry. Soon he'd be packed between the cheeks of her ass, stretching her wide, burning her rim while Jed filled her cunt. The idea precipitated a twinge of longing in her clit as her vagina fluttered with greedy expectation. She stole a glance at Gray's cock, fiercely erect, rising from the nest of black curls darkening his groin. She could feel her damp warmth wetting the inside of her thighs, a humid pool of yearning heating the thick lips of her pussy.

As Jed floated away and opened a narrow compartment on the other side of the cabin, Gray caught Velvet gazing at his cock. The corner of his mouth kicked up into a wickedly sensual smile. Slowly, his hand drifted down to his groin where he wrapped his fingers around his heavy shaft. While Velvet watched with stuttering pulse, he pumped himself provocatively, his hand sliding up and down his length several times before Jed finally rejoined them, a narrow stick clutched in his fingers. Together, they glided across the cabin, Gray leading the way into the sleeping compartment, Jed towing her by the tie looped round her neck.

When they reached the sleeping chamber and Jed finally touched his lips to hers, she moaned with pleasure. Like a woman too long starved of sensation, she clung to the kiss, drinking it down, sampling his delicious male flavor while her lips tingled beneath the sliding press of his hot, wet mouth. His lips were rough silk. His taste was wholly, elementally male.

"Relax," Jed whispered. He brushed his lips into the corner of her mouth then treated himself to a slow, tasting lick. "I'm going to change angle a bit so Gray can kiss you too."

She whimpered into his mouth, a yearning sound of complaint, sucking up to his hard lips as he angled his mouth sideways across hers. His warm, smooth chest pulled away from her breasts, exposing her nipples to the air again. As if reaching for the comfort of his absent chest, her bereft nipples hardened into desperately wanton little spikes. She felt Gray's hands, warm and rough, rounding beneath her bottom and sliding up toward the back of her knees.

When Jed had finished resituating himself, his mouth still covered her lips but his body floated perpendicular to hers.

She squirmed in the air, wanting more than just his mouth covering hers. She wanted his body. She wanted earth and gravity and the wonderful masculine weight of his body bearing down on hers. Her whole being was on fire, needing to be rubbed and stroked and loved, weighted down and dominated.

"Relax," he whispered again. "Here comes Gray."

Forcing herself to relax, she let her knees curl into her chest. She fed a groan into his mouth, wondering how Gray was going to get to her lips while Jed was monopolizing her mouth so completely. But Gray wasn't after her mouth. His hard hands grasped her behind the knees and pulled her legs open. She felt his thick brush of hair between her thighs. She cried into Jed's mouth when Gray's lips opened on her sex. With his fingers wrapped around her thighs just above her knees and his mouth hot on her parted sex, Gray gave her open pussy a long, liquid kiss.

In an absolute paroxysm of pleasure, Velvet tossed her head instinctively, causing her body to undulate on the air. But Jed's hand cupped her nape, restraining her, holding her in place for his next kiss. He panted into her mouth as he bruised her lips against her teeth then gave her his tongue.

His tongue was rough velvet inside her mouth. Hot and hard and demandingly male. She tangled tongues with him, taunting him with a minx-like need to test the power of his passion, pushing her tongue against his, playfully trying to expel his tongue from her mouth. He murmured with pleasure as he pushed savagely back. When his tongue slid around hers and went to the back of her throat, she gathered her tongue into a tight ball and attacked again. Again he slapped her tongue with his, bullying her into submission, dominating her mouth.

Her back arched with pleasure as she yielded to the pure masculine strength of his kiss.

Jed grunted into her mouth. "You're a delicious little tease," he murmured softly. He pulled his face away and gazed down at her from half-closed eyes. "Aren't you?"

She gave him an impish smile.

One eyebrow arched sensually as he gave her a look of primitive hunger. "You won't be smiling when we're finished with you," he warned her in a sexy rumble.

"What's she doing?" Gray mumbled from between her legs.

"She's fighting me," Jed answered, his voice thick with carnal lust. "Why don't you teach her a lesson?"

Gray grunted, his lips vibrating deliciously as they slid on the wet surface of her pussy lips. "What did you have in mind?"

"How about a good tongue-lashing?" he suggested in a warm, rough drawl. "Let's see how hard she fights my tongue when she's spilling out all over yours."

Velvet stared up at him, her lips parting softly as her breath washed out over her damp lips. "Oh, Jed," she whispered breathlessly.

"Oh, Jed," Gray mimicked her with a gruff chuckle. "Let's see if we can change that to 'Oh, Gray'."

"Oh!" she shouted as Gray's mouth sucked up to her open sex. She stilled for him, reveling in the deliciously erotic sensations Gray lavished between her legs. He stroked through her parted folds with a long, lingering lick, curling his tongue around her swollen clit while Jed slid his lips over hers and drove his tongue into her mouth again, daring her to reject his kiss.

Distracted by Gray's tongue swirling through her hungry folds, she gave Jed only a very feeble run for his money, allowing him to subdue her in gradual degrees, succumbing humbly beneath his fierce onslaught, swirling her tongue around his and caressing it submissively. Between her open thighs, she felt Gray's thumbs pulling the rim of her opening wide while he pressed his lips into her folds, gentling her seeping slit with his mouth, feathering his tongue over her clitoris, driving her slowly toward the edge of orgasm. Her cunt spasmed once, shuddering in near completion as Gray taunted her pussy with the hot, wet caress of his tongue.

Velvet grunted out a small choking sound of pleasure. With her fingers knotted in Jed's dark hair, she held on for dear life as she pushed her thighs wider, opening herself for Gray, reveling in the stretch that tautened the muscles of her thighs, panting in small hungry sobs.

She felt Gray's thumbs slipping outside her full, sodden lips, his fingers wet against her skin, tugging her delicate flesh open into a delicious erotic stretch. She waited for the touch of his mouth again—full, hot and ravenous—eating into her pussy.

Gray flicked her clit with the tip of his tongue and she yelped into Jed's mouth.

"Let's see what she has to say now," Gray suggested in a thick baritone.

Jed groaned, obviously loath to uncover her mouth, pursuing her lips aggressively as her head tossed in feverish need.

"Uncover her mouth," Gray ordered roughly.

After another deep groan, Jed relented. His lips were shiny with her wet kisses as his hungry gaze traveled down her sweat-damp body in a carnal caress, his green eyes burning a line of lust between her breasts, across her navel to the damp curls on her mound where Gray's face was buried in her pussy.

Tension rode the taut line of his kiss-damp mouth as Velvet gazed up at him. Flashes of deep color glinted in the richly bronzed waves of his thick, silky hair. His eyes smoldered darkly with desire as he watched Gray working his mouth between her trembling thighs.

Gray's voice was muffled as he spoke against her open sex. "What do you say now, Velvet?"

Velvet groaned and twisted on the air.

Gray kissed her clit, blew on it then lashed it with his tongue.

She gasped.

"I want to hear my name on your lips, Velvet."

"Velvet," Jed murmured between short, raw breaths. "You're going to have to humor the bastard."

"Fuck," Gray rasped. "After making me wait this long, she's going to have to do more than humor me." Gray flattened his tongue over her opening then ran the rough tip around the seeping rim.

Velvet drew in a long, moaning breath. "Jed," she pleaded, "help me."

A damp strand of hair curled down onto his forehead. His eyes moved with a burning sensual urgency down over her belly and into the thatch of curling hair that powdered her mound, sending a flood of moisture from her slit to bathe Gray's lapping tongue. "I'll do what I can," he whispered against her mouth.

She felt Jed's big rough palm slide down her body. His calloused fingers combed through her pubic curls before nudging between the thick lips of her sex.

Gray growled. His tongue slashed across her clit like a jealous dog, attacking Jed's fingers and pushing them out of her pussy. Velvet bucked like a leaf on the wind as the two men fought over the hot pink territory pulsing between her legs.

Bliss. Overwhelming bliss. She hung at the searing edge of orgasm as the two men fought for possession of her plump, hungry clit. She'd never before felt so desired as at that moment, with Jed's finger slipping across her clitoris, stubbornly fighting for the right to pleasure her while Gray's wet tongue dove in to drive him away, claiming her clit with the hot, demanding pressure he forced upon the rumpled little tag of flesh.

Jed's sigh warmed her cheek. He bit gently at her bottom lip. "I'm sorry," he muttered shakily, obviously as aroused as she was by the idea of his fingers in her pussy while Gray's tongue was slipping through her folds. "There's no way around this. You're just gonna have to feed his massive ego."

Velvet moaned in defeat. "Oh, Gray," she croaked.

"Oh, Gray, what?" Gray pushed her relentlessly.

"Oh, Gray, don't stop kissing me," she chanted.

"Are you begging me?" He rubbed his teeth over her clitoris.

She twisted in the air. "Yes, I'm begging you!"

He scraped the blunt edge of his incisors over the hungry flange of flesh.

"*Oh, Gray!*"

"What are you begging me for?"

"To...to let me come, Gray."

"To *let* you come?"

"To *make* me come!"

"That's better," he growled. He rubbed his rough jaw into her open sex, grinding his stubble into her saturated folds.

"Oh, Gray!" she cried. "Oh, Gray! Don't stop! Please, don't stop!"

"You want to come like this?" he murmured. "You want to close and grip and come on empty air...or would you like me to fuck you?" he tempted her before blowing on her sensitive, pulsing nub.

"I...I..."

"Would you like me to fill this sweet little pussy with cock?"

"I...God...Gray...I can't think. Just...just do it now."

Gray let out a lusty, wicked rumble of amusement. "You should see this, Jed. She has a sexy line of sweat beading in the crease between her legs and her pussy. I have her pretty little slit spread wide open, watching her cunt shudder as I blow on her clit."

Jed groaned. "Shut up, you bastard. Either that or trade places."

"No way," Gray answered huskily. "I'm gonna make her come into my mouth and lap her cream up as it spills from her slit."

"Well, just make sure you save some for me," Jed panted. "You going to do it now?"

Gray rimmed her open vulva with his tongue again and Velvet's vagina shuddered, grasping once, twice, three times at empty air before settling down again into a voracious, wide-open, fuck-me-now demand for cock.

"Not quite yet," Gray answered in a taunting growl. "Give me your hands, Velvet."

"Gray?" she murmured.

"Give me you hands," he demanded.

As if seeking safe harbor in his thick locks, Velvet's fingers clenched and knotted and held tight in Jed's hair. But the Cajun reached up and eased her grip open with his thumbs.

"Jed?" she entreated, feeling suddenly small and vulnerable as the two men worked together to manipulate her actions and dominate her body.

Without answering, Jed brushed his lips over her knuckles then moved her hands down her body toward Gray. Gray took her hands and stroked his thumbs into her palms, uncurling her fingers.

"Spread your pussy open for me," he commanded softly.

Her fingers fluttered uncertainly as she plucked at the curls on her mound.

"Open your lips with your fingers," he growled huskily. "I want to see your fingers spreading your sex, Velvet."

Jed rubbed his lips into the corner of her mouth. "Please, Velvet."

Velvet groaned as her fingers dipped into the warm cleft. Her lips were fat and soft, swimming in slippery juices where her dewy essence clung to her heated skin. Carefully, she parted her lips for Gray's devouring gaze.

"Wider," he whispered, his voice scraping with hunger.

She pulled her lips open, baring everything between the thick sodden lips of her sex.

"That's it," he muttered roughly. "I don't know what I like more, Jed — the taste or the texture, the feel of her cunt clasping my tongue or the sight of her moisture easing from her slit — the flavor of her sweet liquid release or her fingers holding her slit open for me so I can watch her opening shudder with need."

Jed nuzzled his face against her cheek. "Want to drive him crazy?" he whispered.

Holding her breath, Velvet nodded up at him.

"Finger your clit," he suggested in a voice strung taut with dark excitement.

She hesitated, though a rush of edgy, yearning need robbed her of breath.

"You're going to love this," Jed assured her in a soft murmur. "You're going to love what you do to us when we see your hands in your pussy. We're giving you permission to share this with us, Velvet. A chance to understand that we love you...with all your shy inhibitions. With all your darkest desires. Do this for us and do this for yourself. Let Gray see your fingers stroking through your folds, playing with your clit while he watches. It'll drive the man insane."

Velvet dipped one finger between her labia and slid it over her clit. Shimmers of pleasure tightened her buttocks and flashed up her spine as she arched and cried out in pleasure.

"Oh, baby," Gray groaned. His shoulders shifted as he reached for his cock. "That's the most beautiful thing I've ever seen. Keep playing with your clit, Velvet. Show me your favorite spot. Show me where you want me to put my mouth, beautiful."

Velvet swirled a finger over the agonized center of her need.

"That's it," Gray rasped, his voice strained. "Jed. Do me a favor and give one of her tits a little squeeze."

Jed's fingers cupped her small round breast. His thumb grazed over her excited nipple before he squeezed the dainty pebbled flesh between thumb and forefinger.

Velvet bucked on the air. "Oh. God. Oh. Gray. Oh. Jed," she sang as both men watched her with burning eyes and rapt expressions.

"Get ready," Gray warned Jed breathlessly.

Jed drove his tongue deep into Velvet's mouth, stifling her cries as Gray covered her sex with his mouth and sucked hard. He rubbed his tongue into the flesh beneath her clit while he sucked the fragile flange of flesh with unrelenting ferocity. Velvet thrashed the air as she held her sex open for him—and orgasmed. Her body sang with mad, wicked pleasure as Gray drew her climax on and on and Jed crushed his mouth against hers, both men gripping her tightly in their big hands, trying to restrain her body as she whipped the air.

"Mmmm," Gray murmured, lapping at the base of her vulva, then trailing his tongue up through her used folds—tender and achingly sensitive—rubbing his tongue into her clit. "What do you say to that, Velvet?"

"I say...it's time for lesson number two," she murmured on a long, contented sigh.

Chapter Twelve

ဆာ

"Jeezis Skies," Gray murmured, "she's a glutton for punishment, isn't she, Jed?"

Velvet giggled deeply. "If that's your idea of punishment, Gray…"

"*Gray.*" Jed interrupted their banter, his voice raw with urgency.

"Right," Gray said, his own voice deepened with desire. "Trade places."

Jed brushed his lips over her mouth. "Keep your fingers where they are," he told her, "holding your pussy open for me."

A second later, Jed's mouth joined with her sex, closing over the tender flesh still heated with Gray's breath, still shuddering with the sweet aftershocks of the climax he'd pushed on her, still slippery with the release that had rushed from her slit to spill into his mouth.

Jed's hands gripped her thighs strongly, pulling her legs against his warm chest. But unlike the bold, demanding press of Gray's mouth, his lips were soft and loving as he pulled his tongue gently up through her pussy, sliding through the delicate ruts where Gray's rough tongue had recently cavorted, collecting her moisture into his mouth and tasting her essence in short, savoring sips.

Angling his face over hers, Gray opened her mouth with his, his lips flavored with her cream, his tongue rubbing it into hers before he trailed his rough, damp jaw over her cheek and beneath her ear as he pulled himself around behind her. She felt the fine, damp skin of his cock drag across the cheeks of her ass then nestle into her crack. With a strong forearm banded around her waist and his free hand palming the sweat-dusted skin between her shoulder blades, he gently forced her to bend at the waist. Then he levered the burning head of his cock downward, prodding between her cheeks while Jed licked up through her folds and settled his tongue near her clit. When Jed flattened his tongue on the swollen nub and pressed, she felt her pulse threading through the tender tag of flesh, throbbing against the pressure of his tongue. Jed fluttered his tongue over the sensitive bundle of nerves a few times then started lapping at it, teasing it, taunting it, painting it with his wet tongue and prodding it from satiated contentment into disturbingly renewed hunger.

While Jed worked his mouth over the rosy folds tucked between Velvet's open thighs, Gray eased his cock head between the cheeks of her ass. With his shank in his hand, he prodded at her anus a few times, savoring the pressure tightening the skin over his wide crown, reveling in the sharp-edged bite of need that hardened his balls and turned his shaft to steel. His chest felt tight as his lungs burned. His heart pounded and his cock throbbed with a demanding need to sheathe itself inside a woman — this woman — and ride her with a savage, driving run to completion.

Velvet's Adept body stunned him in the next instant when the tight ring of her ass opened a minute fraction. With a deliciously arousing view of his cock prodding between her cheeks, he tested the tiny mouth with his broad head. A shining drop of moisture balanced on his slit and he rubbed it into her dark rosebud then painted her puckered rim with the wash of pre-cum that followed. His balls tightened with excitement at the sight of his cock kissing her ass and he reached low to roll his fingers over his rock-hard sac. As he watched, the tiny mouth closed and opened, closed and opened, enticing him to fill that cheeky hole with cock as a heavy pulse of need twisted through his system.

"Don't tempt me," he muttered under his breath. He had one fuck left and he wanted to make it count—twice. He wanted to leave Velvet with the stamp of his cock head on the back of her womb before taking his pleasure inside her tempting little anal opening.

Forgoing the temptation of her ass for the time being, he wrapped her silky locks in his fist and pulled her back against his chest. He tightened the fingers threaded through her hair, grazing his teeth along the tender column of her throat as her neck stretched beneath his mouth, offering him more. He nipped at the moist perfection of her pale skin then loosened his grasp on her hair. With his cock in his hand, he slid his wide dark head down to her wet slit. He swabbed at her notch, letting her sex juices paint his cock head with a gleaming coat of moisture then settled into her vulva and prepared to enter her.

He gasped when Jed's tongue drove against the front of his shaft, right beneath the mushrooming ridge of his cock head, forcing him out of Velvet's luscious, warm hold. "Fuck," he cursed, grasping his thick shank and driving his blunt tip back into place.

Again, Jed attacked with his tongue, lashing at him with savagely disabling swipes that had his cock throbbing and pulsing on the edge of ejaculation. Jed was fighting dirty, slashing at the rim of his crown where he was most sensitive. A telltale burn grew at the back of his balls and Gray clamped his fingers around the thick root, stemming the tide of cum that threatened to surge from his balls and shoot up his shaft.

He growled a deep warning. "Let me in," he rumbled. Releasing his shaft, he reached between Velvet's legs and grasped Jed's chin. He drove his hips forward, bumping his fat cock head against the Cajun's lips. "It's either *her* cunt or *your* mouth, Jed. Take your pick."

Jed had him riding a hard, hungry edge of sexual aggression mixed with anger and frustration—along with a very male drive to get fucked. Despite the fact that Gray had never in his lifetime been remotely attracted to a man, he was ready to follow through with his threat. More than ready, he realized, surprised at just how badly he wanted to push his cock into Jed's hard mouth—if only to put Jed in his place and to be able to claim mastery of the situation.

Jed swiped his tongue over the slippery head of Gray's cock, making his gut clench and his balls prickle with a not altogether unpleasant wave of arousal. He'd never imagined this kind of situation would make him feel so...savagely male, yet there was no denying that a pure, potent exhilaration was firing through his blood at the idea of making Jed take his cock down his throat while Velvet *destroyed* the arrogant Cajun with the feel of her cunt wrapped around his raging hard-on.

Gray shook his head to clear the powerful image, nearly crying out when Jed nipped the fat head of his shaft with his teeth.

"You want in?" the Cajun growled, clearly challenging him. "You wait your fucking turn."

A warning male rumble sounded from deep in Gray's chest. "I'm *saying* it's my turn."

"And I'm saying I'm not done tasting her."

Gray gave in with a vicious obscenity, feeding his rough breath into Velvet's ear and swiping his tongue across the delicate shell he moistened with his raw, panting breath. When Jed was *finally* done tasting, Gray quickly fed his long, throbbing inches into Velvet's slick channel. The Cajun reversed his body over Velvet's, tonguing her clit while his shaft stretched a few inches from her face.

"Time to anchor," Gray announced. "Give us a push."

As Gray's back bumped up against the soft, air-quilted wall, he grasped at one of the stretchy restraints. Holding himself against the wall, he fed his feet through two of the flexible bands. After securing his ankles, he slipped his arms through two more restraints at his sides, working his arms down into the bands until the clear plastech strained over his bulging biceps. Now Gray was anchored to the wall and Velvet was anchored to him, impaled on the long-veined shaft he had buried deep inside her pussy.

Gray took a sharp, gasping breath, almost overwhelmed by the urgent need riding him with vicious intensity. He quelled the urge to move, to thrust, to fuck, wanting to experience Velvet's climax squeezing the hell out of his cock at least once before he took his own release and exploded inside her, expelling his cum into her deliciously hot body. "Okay," Gray panted at Jed. "Your turn to make her come."

Using one of the restraining bands as a pivot point, Jed swung out over Velvet, his face aligned with her pussy, his erection waving in front of her mouth. "If that's what you want," Jed answered, "you're going to have to help me get my cock near her mouth."

Reaching out, Gray wrapped his fingers around the Cajun's shaft and brought it to within inches of Velvet's mouth. He snorted softly. He could hardly believe he had another man's dick in his fist. He'd come a long way since the three of them were cramped together on the Tauran freighter.

"What do you say?" Gray taunted the Cajun. He tightened his grip around Jed's shaft and watched as a pearly drop of pre-cum beaded on his slit. He frowned at the drop of moisture for a moment. "Lick him off," he commanded Velvet in a rough whisper, then pulled Jed's cock close to Velvet's mouth.

She licked the drop away before it could float off.

"What do you *say*?" Gray repeated.

Jed grunted. "I say...get me inside her mouth before I come in your face."

Gray snorted out a soft sound of amusement. Guiding Jed's shaft to Velvet's mouth, he rubbed the flushed wet head over her lips then watched jealously as Velvet opened her mouth and took in the top few inches of Jed's taut shaft. "Don't choke her," he growled as he watched Velvet work her mouth over his ruddy cock. Her mouth slid back, releasing several long, thick inches of Jed's wet shaft. Her tongue flicked out to lick him, the pink tip pale against Jed's dark skin.

Gray groaned as he watched her.

"And pay attention," he added with a growl when he realized Jed had stilled to enjoy Velvet's mouth on his cock instead of working his tongue over her clit. Straining his arms forward, he pulled Jed's face tightly into Velvet's pussy. He watched the pair as their actions became less focused, Velvet's mouth growing slack as she approached orgasm, Jed's hips undulating instinctively in an erotic male rhythm, causing his wet cock head to slip from her loose mouth.

With one hand wrapped around the back of Jed's head and the other grasping his cock, Gray fed the Cajun's shaft back into Velvet's mouth, then clamped her chin into place as she tongued Jed's cock absently.

He rubbed his lips into the delicate shell of her ear. "Hey," he chided her gently. "You pay attention too."

She nodded once, the wet tip of her tongue trailing beneath the ridge on Jed's cock head.

Jed groaned. "Take more of me, Velvet. Take more of me in your mouth, beautiful."

Gray cased her jaw in the cup of his palm, holding it in place for Jed while he rocked more of his cock between her lips and breathed out a long, grating sound of pleasure.

"What's he doing to you now?" Gray murmured against Velvet's ear.

She shook her head, unable to answer with her mouth full of cock.

Reaching up, Gray eased Jed's shaft from her mouth, running the wide, dark tip around her lips. "What's he doing to you with his mouth?" he asked.

"Ohhhh," she breathed. "He's kissing me."

"He's kissing your clit?"

"Y-Yes," she whimpered. "He's kissing me everywhere."

"Who's fucking your cunt?"

She nodded distractedly.

"Who's fucking your cunt, baby?"

She bucked in his arms. "You are!" she cried.

"Damn right," he murmured.

Jed's cock was seeping at the slit again and Gray wiped his pre-cum around her open mouth, bathing the delicate rose surface of her lips with a glistening coat of moisture. When he was done, her lips shone petal-soft and glossy. He'd never seen anything so kissable before in his life, or so fuckable. He wished it were his cock resting against her lips, instead of Jed's.

If he ever got out of this alive, things would be different. In the meantime, a man couldn't have everything. Or at least not everything all at once. He had her fragile pink pussy wrapped around his cock and he was just going to have to make the best of the situation. Surprisingly, he didn't find it entirely unarousing, watching Jed with his cock in Velvet's mouth. It helped that he was the one controlling the situation.

"I think Jed wants to fuck your mouth," he whispered. "I'm going to put his cock back between your lips. Does that sound good to you?"

"Yes," she moaned.

"You want him to fuck your mouth?"

"Yes," she sobbed.

"If I give you his cock will you do something for me in return?"

She swallowed and licked her lips, her tongue darting over the glossy sheen that painted her lips. "What...what do you want me to do, Gray?"

"I want you to come," he murmured. "I want to feel you close around my cock as Jed is fucking your mouth and sucking on your sweet, syrupy little clit."

"O-Okay," she answered breathlessly, her eyes huge as she eyed Jed's brutally dark shaft.

With his hand gripping Jed's cock, Gray fed it between her lips.

"Ahhh," he rumbled out on a sigh deep with pleasure. He closed his eyes as he felt Velvet's pussy clamp along his cock. "God, that's beautiful," he groaned as she closed up around him, bruising his painfully used flesh in a long sequence of throttling contractions. "Keep coming," he muttered. "Just keep on coming, Velvet."

She came for endlessly long seconds as Jed played his tongue over her sex, teasing a never-ending stream of contractions out of her climaxing pussy, his tongue threading through her thick folds and flattening her sensitive clit, staying with her though she bucked against his mouth. The tip of his tongue grazed across the wide base of Gray's cock a few times as he went after those last fluttering contractions.

Gray grunted as his balls hardened with every audacious swipe of Jed's tongue. He didn't think the Cajun was *trying* to lick his cock. On the other hand, he didn't think Jed was trying very hard not to. But the bastard was testing him with every daring lick. Gray buried his teeth in his bottom lip, almost drawing blood as he fought the burning need to release, damned if he was going to let Jed make him come.

"Keep her coming, Jed," he croaked perversely. He could take it. He could take it all, he told himself as sweat burst from his pores and beaded on his heated skin.

Jed delivered. The Cajun didn't pull his mouth from Velvet's thick folds until the final shivering tremor of her orgasm was rippling around Gray's shaft. By that time, Gray's skin was coated with a glistening sheen of blistering hot sweat.

"By the Princess," Jed complained in a deep grumble as he reversed himself on her body again. "I almost lost it when you started talking about my cock in her mouth."

169

"That's what you were supposed to do, you ignorant outlander."

"Ignorant? I'm not ignorant. I just didn't want to come. Not yet."

Gray opened his eyes on the Cajun's green gaze. "Now you know how I felt."

"Did we get you close?" Jed asked with a satyr's smile.

Gray let his lips curl upward. "Jeezis" was his only answer.

Jed continued, his voice rough and soft. "I want to be inside her with you when we come—all three of us together."

"One more time with love?" Gray suggested after a moment's silence.

"That's right," said Jed, his voice quiet with emotion. "One more time with love."

Gray nodded. "Let's turn her around. I want to show you something first."

Lifting Velvet off his cock, he turned her around so that she faced him. He gazed at her mouth longingly, hesitating a moment before rubbing his mouth into hers. Her lips were soft, a damp heaven beneath his own. He tasted Jed's hunger painted across her mouth—sharp and musky and male. Because it was a part of her, having sex with her and loving her, he swallowed it down with an eager groan breaking from his throat. The taste of Jed's cum on his lips was a stark reminder of his own carnal need, gnawing at his gut, burning in his shaft and aching in his balls.

Jed's eyes snagged his gaze as Gray pulled away from Velvet's moist mouth. His green eyes glowed in masculine understanding, a sensual smile flickering at the edge of his mouth.

With his gaze attached to Jed's, Gray bent Velvet at the waist again, guiding her face down his chest this time. "Rub your dick into her ass."

Jed shook his head uncertainly. "What?"

"Just do it," Gray insisted quietly, reaching back for Velvet's cheeks and pulling them open.

Jed pulled his cock head through her crease, grunting with surprise. With his thumbs covering Gray's fingers, he pulled her cheeks wider, watching her anus open perhaps half a centimeter. "Oh, man," he breathed in amazement. "She's opening for me. Isn't that just the cheekiest damn thing you've ever seen?"

Gray chuckled softly. "She's asking for it."

"Asking for it, nothing! She's begging for it!"

"Think I could get the hammer in there?"

"I think we could *both* probably get in there one day!" Jed murmured with rough male delight.

Gray groaned at the thought then sighed.

What a time to die.

He shook off the heavy weight of melancholy. "Would you like that, Velvet? Both of us packing your ass?"

"Mmmm," she answered languidly as she nibbled at one of his nipples. "I think I'd rather have you both packed inside my pussy."

Gray grunted, imagining his shaft sliding up Jed's length as both men drove into her sleek, wet channel. "Hadn't thought of that."

Jed took a long shallow breath. "Air's getting thin in here," he pointed out.

"We'd better finish up," Gray agreed with a grunt.

"I got your back door," Jed volunteered.

"Not this time," he growled. "This time her little buttonhole is mine."

Again, Gray turned Velvet. Jed floated up against her as she straightened in the space between the two men. Gray watched Jed's eyes, hazy with pleasure as he slowly worked his cock into her pussy. "You got the lubestick?" Gray reminded him.

Jed grunted in answer, reaching around behind Velvet and fingering her puckered opening before feeding the stick between her cheeks. Gray watched Jed's prodding fingers for a few seconds, then covered Jed's fingers with his own, pushing the lubricating stick all the way inside her.

He gave her a few minutes for the lubricant to soften and coat her inner walls. Then, with forefinger and thumb clamping his cock just beneath the crown, Gray pressed his head against the enticing little mouth that beckoned him to ream inside. For a few seconds he let her ass nibble at his cock head before forging forward. He got his crown inside her then gasped as that demure-looking mouth clamped viciously around the rim of his hooded bulb. "Jeezis," he croaked, then hurriedly shoved another inch inside her. With a restrained ferocity that had a new sweat breaking out across his heated skin, he forged his way into Velvet's body, gradually filling her ass.

When he was almost buried to the balls, he ran into a kink. He looked down between their bodies, where his damp curls shadowed the root of his cock and his wide base stretched her delicate opening impossibly wide. He panted as he dragged his lips into her nape. His heart, exploding with a blend of carnal lust and wrenchingly tender devotion, felt like it might burst from his chest. He groaned into the tiny hairs feathering her nape. "Sweetheart," he rasped from between clenched teeth, "are you sure you can take this?"

Her ring clenched at his words, biting into the veins that snaked up his cock. Jed groaned at the same time. Her vagina had probably given him a vicious once-over as well.

"I can take it," she whispered as she lifted her mouth to Jed. As Gray watched, Jed kissed her rapaciously while Velvet's sex fluttered with excitement.

"She can take it," Jed panted, breaking his lips from her mouth. "Just...get in there before I come without you."

172

"Okay, give me a minute," Gray rasped as he worked at the stubborn twist, prodding gently but insistently until her body allowed his heavy shaft to penetrate that final intimate inch. Now the fragile membrane lining her vagina was all that separated his pulsing shaft from Jed's thick cock.

With his cock deeply seated inside Velvet's rear, his balls resting warm and rough against Jed's testicles, he murmured a deep sound of pleasure. Jed returned his heated gaze with a look of consummate understanding mixed with deep yearning.

Gray wrapped his hand around Velvet's slender neck. His fingers curled over her windpipe while his thumb gripped her nape below the hairline. When he put a wet breath against her ear, he felt Jed's hand slide around the back of her neck. Jed's fingers cradled her nape below Gray's thumb while he rubbed his thumb into the hollow at the base of her throat.

Together, the men held her fragile life cupped in their hands.

Gray groaned as he savored her scattered pulse drumming against his fingers. His cock throbbed hugely within her tightly cinched ring as her delicate heartbeat fluttered in his grip. He experienced a deliciously arousing feeling of eroticism — a male mixture of power tempered with tenderness. It was this fragile vulnerability on the part of a woman that made a man feel so potent, so strong. At that moment in time, this woman's life belonged to the men in whose hands she'd placed herself — despite any independence she might wish to claim. They held it in their hands! It was theirs to crush or to treasure. Theirs to destroy or protect. It was a breath-stealing moment of eroticism that only another man would understand.

Gray pulled his lips away from beneath Velvet's ear and checked Jed's burning gaze. There, in Jed's eyes, he saw reflected his own carnal desire. With his eyes locked on Jed, he tightened his fingers a hairsbreadth and watched as his wing companion did the same.

Velvet rewarded the men with a deep murmur of pleasure. Her eyes were almost black. Only a thin edge of amethyst rimmed her wide pupils. Gray smiled breathlessly as her body quivered around his cock where he penetrated her. From all appearances, the little Adept was aroused by this demonstration of masculine power—her lovers' hard fingers shackling her throat with male strength.

Gray narrowed his gaze on Jed. Simultaneously, the two men loosened their grip, soothing Velvet's satiny pale flesh beneath their fingers, worshipping her skin, thanking her for allowing them this intimate liberty.

"Ready to get fucked?" Gray murmured, sucking vainly for a full lungful of air.

"Ready," Jed confirmed in a raw whisper. He dipped his head and dragged his lips across the faint pink marks that they'd left slashing across Velvet's throat.

"Velvet?" Gray asked.

"Ready," she answered on an edgy, shivering sigh.

Together, the two wing companions took their last woman. With strong, driving surges they filled her, holding deep inside her for a full second before pulling their hips and thrusting into her again. Between their bodies, she writhed and whimpered, kissing first Jed, then turning her head and giving her lips to Gray.

Gray's breaths were short and shallow, as he tried to fill his lungs. Velvet's unbearably tight noose wrapped his cock like a savage garrote, cutting into his blood flow, traveling up to the rim of his crown as he pulled his shaft, then scraping back down his thick, trembling length before choking him mercilessly just above the balls. "Tell us when, beautiful. We're just waiting for you."

When she gave them the word, they came.

Gray choked on the obscene words of pleasure that spilled from his mouth. As he started to climax, her tight clenching ring kept him at bay, squeezing him off at the root in vicious spasms, stringing out his orgasm as his ejaculate fought its way out of his balls and spat to fill her ass in erratically jetting spurts.

"Oh. My. God!" he roared, burying his face in the curve between her neck and shoulder. At the edges of his blurred consciousness, he heard Jed shouting Gray's name as well as Velvet's, mixing them together in deep, guttural grunts of pleasure.

Afterward, they remained plastered together against the quilted wall of the sleeping compartment, their sex-heated bodies sealed together with a damp sheen of sweat. The air was thin and getting thinner with each breath Gray drew into his lungs. He resisted the urge to gasp—it wouldn't do any good and would only underline their fate. He didn't want to upset either of his companions.

His lovers.

Jed caught his eye. "Good idea?" he whispered.

"Good idea," Gray sighed in confirmation. "Two in one. Three simultaneous orgasms. I'm glad you suggested it."

He brushed his lips over Velvet's mouth, struggling to keep his eyes open. He drew in a long breath and ignored the fact that it didn't seem to help. "Say hello to Jason and Match for us."

"What?" she whispered. "No. No, Gray."

Gray smiled, feeling like he'd finally gotten it right, glad that he'd thought of it before Jed had. He looked at Jed, who was smiling. Well, at least he'd mentioned it before Jed. It was damn hard to stay ahead of the Cajun.

"You'll make it," Jed told her, rubbing his lips into her neck below her ear. "You're an Adept. Somehow, your body will adjust to the diminishing levels of oxygen. The change will be gradual enough."

At Jed's words, a surge of panic crushed into Velvet's heart. She hadn't planned on surviving! At this point, it was less painful to think she'd die in her sleep, along with her two lovers, than to think she might live without them.

Jed lifted her chin with his finger. "After we fall asleep," he murmured, "while you're waiting for Jason and Match, I want you to get a notebook out of the supply drawer."

Velvet's heart thudded dully in her chest. She knew what Jed was up to. If he could extract a promise from her, no matter how insignificant, he could *require* her to continue her life without them. Her chin trembled and she sucked in her bottom lip. She *would not* cry. She was Spaceforce! "You want me to draw you?" she croaked.

He shook his head. "Draw yourself," he whispered. "Keep *yourself* alive, Velvet. Do you understand? Keep yourself alive the same way you kept your friends alive. Your friends from Etiens."

She looked away, blinking back the pressure of hot tears.

"Promise me, Velvet."

She jerked her chin. "I promise." One renegade tear burned a trail down her cheek and curled beneath her jaw. She forced a smile as she returned Jed's gaze.

He smiled quietly back at her. "Tell her you love her, Gray."

Gray answered gruffly, "She already knows I love her."

Jed closed his eyes and took a long breath of thin air. "Okay. I'll tell her for you," he murmured. "I love you, Velvet." He put his lips against hers but was asleep before he finished the kiss. Despite her promise to Jed, Velvet felt the switch click into the off position.

She turned her head toward Gray, feeling blank and quiet inside. Ominously quiet and empty. "Any last requests, Gray?"

He gave her a long careful look before he sighed. "You'll find some clothes in the compartment marked personal, out in the main cabin. I'd like to die with dignity," he said with a lopsided smile. "There should be something in there that will fit Jed as well. Maybe an extra shirt for you."

"You want to die with your boots on?" she asked him with a sad smile.

He snorted out a dry chuckle of amusement. "Well, I'd like to die with my pants on, at least." His expression grew solemn again as he reached out a hand and ruffled it through Jed's tousled locks. His voice was rough as he added, "And I'd like to see you smile once more before I close my eyes."

She smiled. Twisting her neck to meet his lips, she kissed him.

When Gray's mouth turned slack beneath hers, she disentangled herself from her lovers. In the main cabin, she found the compartment Gray had spoken of. Clamped inside she found a small supply of men's clothing. Although she searched the surrounding drawers and closets, she failed to locate a spare pair of boots.

Returning to the sleeping compartment, she towed first Gray then Jed back to the main cabin. There, she used the ship's bidet to clean the men. Using the male attachment, she clamped the flexible mouth over Jed's penis while the bidet sucked water over his cock and expelled it out into space. By the time she finished doing the same for Gray, the hammer was semi-rigid.

She shook her head as she eyed Gray's cock with a feeling of vague melancholy. Typical Gray. If the lieutenant couldn't die with his boots on, he would at least die with a hard-on.

The men were still warm as she dressed them—still alive—though their pulses were sluggish and their breathing barely detectable. Dressing a limp man floating in zero gravity was very much like trying to push a string but eventually she had them garbed in clean cock pockets, civilian pants and non-regulation T-shirts.

After changing out the bidet's attachment, she cleaned herself and dressed in one of Gray's T-shirts which would have been long enough to cover her bottom, had there been any gravity to pull it down. Although she used her olive drab tie to secure it around her waist, the soft white T-shirt persisted in floating up over her hips. Fortunately, she found a crisp, clean pair of boxers. The pink hearts suggested they'd been a gift from a previous admirer. Evidently, the feelings hadn't been *too* strongly reciprocated — the pink and white shorts had never been worn.

Covered up, if not dressed, Velvet returned to the sleeping compartment. With a small utility dagger clutched in her fist, she slashed open every single pillow on the cushioned walls, allowing the air trapped within the quilting to circulate throughout the cabin. Then she checked on the men before she strapped herself into one of the command seats and settled down with a notebook to wait for Lieutenants Orlov and Maloney.

Her lovers were still breathing, though only just.

* * * * *

Velvet was asleep when she heard the deep, low boom of a hatch connection. It would take a minute or two before Jason and Matchstick completed the hookup. She squeezed her eyes together, unwilling to look at her two lovers, feeling thankfully empty, relieved that she had no emotions with which to grieve.

She wasn't sure she would survive if she did.

A groan interrupted her blank musings. When she opened her eyes, she saw Gray's hands moving up to hold his head. Releasing her restraints, she gathered her feet beneath her and shot out of the chair. Jed was moaning as well, looking groggy and red-eyed. She stared at the two men in wonder.

"Why the *fuck* am I still alive?" Gray complained. "Jeezis. My head hurts like a son of a bitch."

"Oxygen deprivation," Jed moaned, looking just as miserable.

178

They were alive. Both of them. Gray and Jed were alive.

The hatch door swung open and Jason floated through the portal, white as a ghost, obviously terrified to face what he was sure he would find—three dead bodies floating inside the Hexapod. "Velvet," he said, stunned. Then, "Gray!" he shouted. "Jed! What the hell?"

"Hey," Gray smiled at him. "Did you bring any oxygen with you?"

Matchstick was right behind Jason. Together they towed first Jed then Gray into their pod. Velvet clutched Gray's arm and followed. Jason closed the hatch behind her, sealing behind them Gray's Hex and the carbon dioxide-laden air.

Gray rubbed his face and eyes, gulping in huge lungfuls of delicious oxygen-rich air. Even though his brain was barely functioning, he knew the instant Velvet loosened her grip on his arm. Turning his head, he looked for her. He frowned as she drifted limply away. "Velvet," he called.

She didn't answer.

"Jason, Match! Something's wrong with Velvet." Gray tried to get to her but Jason reached her first.

"She's not breathing," Jason shouted. "She's unconscious. Match, get her an oxygen mask!"

Gray's head was in a heavy fog as he dragged himself over to her. "Jeezis, what's wrong with her? Match!" Matchstick put a mask in his hands and Gray clamped it over her mouth. "Come on," he grated, watching Velvet's still features.

"No!" Suddenly, Jed was beside him, tearing the mask away from her face.

"What!" Gray roared. "What are you doing?" As Gray watched, Jed pinched Velvet's nose and covered her mouth with his. "Are you crazy?" Gray howled.

179

Jed sucked in another quick lungful of air and held it for a second before he blew it into Velvet's lungs. "Get the door open on our pod," he commanded before he sucked in a third breath.

Slowly, the gears started turning in Gray's head. "Oh, shit." he groaned. "Jason! Open our Hex. Velvet's going back in."

"What?"

"I'll let Jed explain," he answered gruffly. "Okay, Jed. My turn."

As Gray administered the kiss of life to the love of his life, Jed explained, "We never ran out of oxygen. That's why we're still alive. We should have run out six hours ago. As the oxygen in the cabin decreased, the carbon dioxide increased. But the change was gradual enough for Velvet to adapt. Her lungs adjusted so that she could breathe the carbon dioxide." Jed nodded, his gaze soft as he considered her fluttering eyelids. "So while Velvet was breathing in carbon dioxide, guess what she was breathing out?"

Jason stared. "Oxygen," he murmured in quiet revelation.

Jed nodded. "Like other organisms that absorb carbon dioxide, her lungs were expelling oxygen. Enough to keep Gray and me alive. Eventually the cabin reached some sort of balance. There was enough oxygen for us to survive on while, at the same time, Velvet was living on the carbon dioxide that we were exhaling. When you dragged us inside your Hex, she couldn't breathe because there wasn't enough carbon dioxide in your pod's atmosphere. That's why I gave her artificial respiration. Every breath I expel is a mixture of oxygen and carbon dioxide."

Jason kept nodding and smiling as he watched Gray with Velvet. "That's amazing," he kept saying. "Amazing! Are you guys gonna give her artificial all the way back to Earth Base Ten?"

Jed laughed. "Let's put her back in Gray's Hex and gradually feed her oxygen until her lungs readjust back to normal. Rig me up with an oxygen mask and I'll go with her."

Gray lifted his head long enough to growl, "Like hell you will." When Jed glared at him, Gray relented. "Not without me, at any rate."

Chapter Thirteen

๛

Jed kicked back in his chair and stretched his long legs before him. "So," he concluded for the benefit of his audience, "the Grundian High Command is history. Velvet saved our lives. I saved Velvet's life. Happy endings all around," he uttered with an indolent smirk.

He and Velvet, along with his three wing companions, were crowded around one end of a table in a brew house on Delta Base Twenty. They'd made the detour to the space station hoping to find Jed's eYonan friends still onstation. Junkie and his lot filled out the sides of the long beer-stained table. Only Jason was quiet as he flipped through the pages of Velvet's sketchbook.

Gray scowled at the Cajun. "Aren't you leaving something out?" he growled.

"Gray managed to keep out of the way," Jed added with a lazy grin.

"And somehow managed to save your life at the same time," Gray pointed out, "when you were choking to death on the Grundian space station."

"If you like," Jed conceded. He lifted his beer in a casual salute to his wing leader. "Now that it's all over, aren't you glad you didn't space me?"

"Only at times," Gray answered.

"Only at times?"

"In very widely spaced intervals," Gray growled. He snaked an arm around Velvet's shoulders and pulled her into his hard frame.

Jed was seated on her other side. Not to be outdone, he slid his palm across the table and wrapped his fingers around her hand. "Is that how they're wearing their hair on eYona these days?" he put to Olan.

"That's how they're wearing it if they're musicians," Olan replied, riffing a hand back through his shoulder-length blond curls. His face shone with admiration as his gaze settled on Velvet. He jabbed his elbow into Junkie's side. "Maybe we should find *us* a woman and settle down."

Junkie pulled his eyes from the sketch Jason was looking at. His eyebrows shot upward. "*Us*? What do you mean, *us*?"

"I mean *us*. You. Me. Fucking a beautiful woman."

"I don't need your help to fuck a woman," Junkie scoffed.

Olan winked at his eYonan companions. "Nah. You just need help identifying 'em."

Junkie rolled his eyes as he slumped in his chair. "Oh! Here we go," he grumbled. "I never fucked that 'droid in Geveena."

"'Course you didn't," Olan taunted. "Although you probably would have if she'd had any working parts."

Junkie laughed. "You're never gonna let me live that down, are you?"

"Not if I can *possibly* help it," Olan answered agreeably.

"That's one of the reasons I'd never consider doubling up with you," Junkie informed him.

"*One* of the reasons? You got a list going?"

Junkie glanced across the table at Jason, catching his eye and giving him a quick wink. "If I were going to share a woman with another man, I'd probably pick an Earther as second man in."

"What? I'm offended!" Olan exclaimed, smacking his hand over his heart while choking back his amusement.

"*You're* offended?" Jason protested with a cynical snort, "How do you think I feel?"

"Why would you choose an Earther over an old friend like me?" Olan demanded with feigned outrage.

Junkie explained it to him slowly, as though he were a very dim child, "When it's very, very dark and you're in bed together, you can't mistake an Earthman for a woman."

Olan rubbed his smooth chin thoughtfully as he narrowed his eyes on Gray's stubbled jaw. "What if your Earther pal mistakes *you* for a woman?"

"It doesn't work that way," Gray interjected swiftly.

"It doesn't work that way," Jed backed him up loyally.

Olan's eyes narrowed suspiciously. "Uh-huh," he said, his voice thick with sarcasm. Digging his timepiece out of his pocket, he gave Junkie a look that said "time to go".

Junkie pushed back from the table, flipping his thick black braid behind his shoulder as he stood. "We're out of here," he announced before stopping to grasp hands first with Jed, then Gray and Match. Grabbing Velvet's proffered hand, he leaned over and dropped a kiss on her cheek. "What about you guys?"

"We have a couple of rooms here onstation," Jed explained. "We're heading back to Earth after we've rested up. Velvet needs to get back and check in on her sister."

"And I have to start battlespace training," Velvet reminded him.

"That's right," Jed confirmed, turning his face to smile at her. "We gotta get you off the ground and up into space with us."

Junkie loitered beside Jason a moment, gazing down on the sketch that had obviously captured the blond airman's interest. "Who is she?" he asked quietly.

Jason shook his head. "I don't know," he said haltingly. His frown was troubled as he checked Velvet's face then returned his gaze to the drawing.

"Well," Junkie murmured in a rough drawl as Velvet leaned forward to check out the sketch, "if you ever find her...*get in touch with me.*"

"It's Lacey. My sister," Velvet told the men quietly, scanning first Jason's face then the face of the tall dark man who towered over him.

Jason nodded solemnly and closed the notebook as Junkie's friends got to their feet and offered their goodbyes. The outlanders' cleated boots scraped noisily against the hard floors as the tall leather-clad men swaggered toward the exit.

Gray frowned at Junkie's back, his reaction a mixture of jealousy and concern. The tall, rangy eYonan had a lot of brass and it rubbed Gray the wrong way. Junkie would have to be one hell of a strong bastard if he thought he could take on the emotional load of both a shattered Adept and a former Ibeeza Boy.

Jason had issues, issues he'd carried since his youth, issues he'd buried deep in his heart. If Junkie thought he could work out a relationship between the three of them, he'd need a lot of strength...as well as a heart the size of the large galaxy.

Jed's next words didn't exactly convince him that Junkie was the man for the job.

"There goes the biggest womanizer in the quadrant," Jed muttered, following Junkie with his eyes.

"Bigger than this one?" Velvet challenged him while flicking her eyes at Gray.

"Gray doesn't count anymore. He's reformed."

"I'm reformed," Gray agreed with a solemn smile.

"Do you think eYona will be admitted to the Alliance?" Velvet asked.

Jed groaned. "I hope not."

Velvet questioned him with a smile.

Jed lifted his chin toward the brew house door. "If eYona *is* admitted, those guys will be the first to sign on at Spaceforce."

"We'll be eight years ahead of them," Jason reasoned as he smoothed his fingers over the notebook's worn cover.

"Yeah but with their experience, it won't take them long to catch up," Jed pointed out.

"Experience?" Matchstick said, "But...I thought your friends were musicians."

"They *are* musicians...when they're not fighting."

Velvet tilted her head thoughtfully as she considered Jed's statement. "Then those swords on their belts...aren't just for show?"

"They're for real," Jed answered. "The planet of eYona never developed projectile weapons. We don't have the necessary natural resources to produce explosive devices. And Inter-Gal rules forbid interplanetary trade of weapons, though that rule will be hard to enforce with the Grundians threatening every galaxy in the lower quadrants. But, yeah. The swords are real and those guys know how to use them."

Velvet smiled suddenly. "Does that mean *you* can fence too?"

Jed pushed back his shoulders. "There isn't a man or woman on the planet of eYona who doesn't know how to use a sword."

"In that case," she told him with a grin lighting her features, "I'd like to cross swords with you someday."

Jed gave her a long, slow smile. "There she is," he murmured, catching Gray's gaze and lifting his chin toward the woman sitting between them.

Gray watched Velvet's face, trying to see what it was that Jed saw in her eyes. Somehow it eluded him.

He could see that she was changing. She was no longer chipped ice *or* diamonds. She was more like...warm opal, shifting and vibrant—more complex with more color, more

186

facets, more depth. There was a new light of excitement in her eyes and a demure blush of heat painted across her cheeks. Even her hair, previously a wash of pale sunshine, was now shot through with bold, fiery strands of red.

Their little Adept was changing...and doing a damn efficient job of it.

And yet...

Gray sighed. In some ways, Jed saw more than Gray ever would. Jed saw more than mere amethyst when he looked in Velvet's eyes. He saw all the way into her soul, all her needs, her strengths, her vulnerabilities. "I wish I could see her the way you do," Gray told him in a quiet murmur.

Jed's slit-eyed gaze was warm green. The smile he returned Gray was almost humble. At least, it was almost humble for the Cajun.

"So," Gray cleared his throat, "the news from home was good?"

Jed lifted one shoulder. "I think so. The eYonan civil war is over. My cousin, Saxon, is married and happy. His band is recording again."

Gray nodded over his beer.

"He and his best friend married an imp together," Jed continued in a voice that betrayed his hope. "Danjer's an Earther," he added almost awkwardly.

Gray nodded again, frowning as he glanced at Jason and Match. "We'll have to visit eYona," he offered carefully.

Jed held his gaze for a few seconds. Finally satisfied with what he saw in Gray's eyes, he pushed back in his chair and stood, pulling Velvet up with him. With an arm around her waist, the Cajun reeled her into his side. "We're going to bed," Jed announced to the table in general. His eyes flicked to Gray. "See you back in the room."

Jason handed the battered notebook up to Velvet. She tucked it under her arm then leaned over Gray to grace his mouth with a long, sweet, lingering kiss. She was smiling back at him as Jed drew her across the room.

Gray's gaze followed the pair out of the brew house.

Velvet wasn't the only one who had changed. Something had changed in Gray as well. He still loved Velvet—loved her passionately, possessively. He'd probably kill any man who tried to lay a finger on her. Any man other than Jed.

Gray wasn't sure when his acceptance of Jed had started, exactly—it had probably been a gradual evolution. Knowing Jed, the sneaky bastard had planned the whole damn thing.

It had probably begun back at Delta Base Twenty where Jed had earned Gray's confidence when he'd marked Velvet with Gray's come. Then in the S.I.S., Jed had started nudging Gray and Velvet back together while quietly staking his own small, understated claim. On the Grundian space station, the three of them had been forced to take a step they'd probably never have taken on their own. That step was reinforced and legitimized when the trio had chosen to consummate their relationship in the Hex. Again, it probably would never have happened if they hadn't thought their hours were numbered but that was beside the point—it *had* happened.

But by far the catalyzing moment occurred when they'd almost lost Velvet—after Jason and Match had arrived to rescue them. In that moment, Gray's feelings for the Cajun had been transformed. When Velvet had been suffocating, Gray hadn't been able save her. Suffering from the worst headache of the century—his brain cells barely firing—he'd been in too much of a panic to think straight. It was Jed who'd saved her life. And for that, Gray would be forever grateful.

For that, Gray would love Jed until his dying day.

Jason frowned and cleared his throat before he ventured a comment. "I guess it was pretty terrible, the things the Grundians made you do?"

Gray smiled wryly. "Yeah. Terrible."

"Think you'll ever be the same again?"

Gray shook his head thoughtfully as he stood. His gaze was on the doorway through which Jed had recently guided Velvet. Would he ever be the same again? Did he even want to be? Each of the three airmen owed each other a debt—the sort of debt it would probably take a full lifetime to repay. Finally, he smiled at his old friend.

"I hope not," he answered. "Jed and I will be marrying Velvet as soon as we can get leave to travel. Will you guys make the trip to eYona with us?"

Jason shared a smile with Matchstick. "An eYonan wedding? We wouldn't miss it for the universe."

About the Author

ഇ

Employed as an engineer, I've worked in an underground mine that went up — inside a mountain. I've swung over the Ohio River in a tiny cage suspended from a crane in the middle of an electrical storm. I've hung over the Hudson River at midnight in an aluminum boat suspended from a floating barge at the height of a blizzard, while snowplows on the bridge overhead rained slush and salt down on my shoulders. You can't do this sort of work without developing a sense of humor and a taste for adventure.

A relative newcomer to the publishing industry, I read my first romance five years ago and decided to try my hand at writing. Both my reading and writing habits are subject to mood and I usually have several stories going at once. When I need a really good idea for a story, I clean toilets. Now there's an activity that engenders escapism.

I was surveying when I met my husband. He was my 'rod man'. While I was trying to get my crosshairs on his stadia rod, he dropped his pants and mooned me. Next thing I know, I've got the backside of paradise in my viewfinder. So I grabbed the walkie-talkie. "That's real nice," I told him, "but would you please turn around? I'd rather see the other side."

It was love at first sight.

Madison welcomes comments from readers. You can find her website and email address on her author bio page at www.ellorascave.com.

Tell Us What You Think

We appreciate hearing reader opinions about our books. You can email us at Comments@EllorasCave.com.

Why an electronic book?

We live in the Information Age — an exciting time in the history of human civilization, in which technology rules supreme and continues to progress in leaps and bounds every minute of every day. For a multitude of reasons, more and more avid literary fans are opting to purchase e-books instead of paper books. The question from those not yet initiated into the world of electronic reading is simply: *Why?*

1. *Price.* An electronic title at Ellora's Cave Publishing and Cerridwen Press runs anywhere from 40% to 75% less than the cover price of the exact same title in paperback format. Why? Basic mathematics and cost. It is less expensive to publish an e-book (no paper and printing, no warehousing and shipping) than it is to publish a paperback, so the savings are passed along to the consumer.

2. *Space.* Running out of room in your house for your books? That is one worry you will never have with electronic books. For a low one-time cost, you can purchase a handheld device specifically designed for e-reading. Many e-readers have large, convenient screens for viewing. Better yet, hundreds of titles can be stored within your new library — on a single microchip. There are a variety of e-readers from different manufacturers. You can also read e-books on your PC or laptop computer. (Please note that Ellora's Cave does not endorse any specific brands.

You can check our websites at www.ellorascave.com or www.cerridwenpress.com for information we make available to new consumers.)

3. *Mobility*. Because your new e-library consists of only a microchip within a small, easily transportable e-reader, your entire cache of books can be taken with you wherever you go.

4. ***Personal Viewing Preferences.*** Are the words you are currently reading too small? Too large? Too… ANNOYING? Paperback books cannot be modified according to personal preferences, but e-books can.

5. ***Instant Gratification.*** Is it the middle of the night and all the bookstores near you are closed? Are you tired of waiting days, sometimes weeks, for bookstores to ship the novels you bought? Ellora's Cave Publishing sells instantaneous downloads twenty-four hours a day, seven days a week, every day of the year. Our webstore is never closed. Our e-book delivery system is 100% automated, meaning your order is filled as soon as you pay for it.

Those are a few of the top reasons why electronic books are replacing paperbacks for many avid readers.

As always, Ellora's Cave and Cerridwen Press welcome your questions and comments. We invite you to email us at Comments@ellorascave.com or write to us directly at Ellora's Cave Publishing Inc., 1056 Home Avenue, Akron, OH 44310-3502.

COMING TO A
BOOKSTORE
NEAR YOU!

ELLORA'S
CAVE

Bestselling Authors Tour

UPDATES AVAILABLE AT
WWW.ELLORASCAVE.COM

MAKE EACH DAY MORE *EXCITING* WITH OUR

ELLORA'S
CAVEMEN
CALENDAR

WWW.ELLORASCAVE.COM

*Discover for yourself why readers can't get enough
of the multiple award-winning publisher
Ellora's Cave.*

*Whether you prefer e-books or paperbacks,
be sure to visit EC on the web at
www.ellorascave.com*

*for an erotic reading experience that will leave you
breathless.*

Printed in Great Britain by
Amazon.co.uk, Ltd.,
Marston Gate.